"You called me be~~cause you're worried,~~ said Zeke. "Clearly I was a last resort."

"Yes," Brooke replied, "because I don't want the detectives to know. I need to finish this case. It's... I need to. If they're worried about threats to me, either I'll get replaced or they'll worry more about new threats than the very important information I'm *this* close to uncovering."

"I thought they knew who killed those people. What more important information could there be?"

She hesitated, because clearly she knew more about the case than he did and she probably shouldn't go sharing the details with just anyone.

But he wasn't *just* anyone.

"If you want me to keep you safe, Brooke, I have to know what I'm keeping you safe from."

COLD CASE
MURDER MYSTERY

NICOLE HELM

INTRIGUE

For those who left us too soon.

H Harlequin®
INTRIGUE™

ISBN-13: 978-1-335-45721-9

Cold Case Murder Mystery

Copyright © 2025 by Nicole Helm

Harlequin Enterprises ULC
22 Adelaide St. West, 41st Floor
Toronto, Ontario M5H 4E3, Canada
www.Harlequin.com

Printed in Lithuania

Recycling programs for this product may not exist in your area.

MIX
Paper | Supporting responsible forestry
FSC® C021394

Nicole Helm grew up with her nose in a book and the dream of one day becoming a writer. Luckily, after a few failed career choices, she gets to follow that dream—writing down-to-earth contemporary romance and romantic suspense. From farmers to cowboys, Midwest to *the* West, Nicole writes stories about people finding themselves and finding love in the process. She lives in Missouri with her husband and two sons, and dreams of someday owning a barn.

Books by Nicole Helm

Harlequin Intrigue

Hudson Sibling Solutions

Cold Case Kidnapping
Cold Case Identity
Cold Case Investigation
Cold Case Scandal
Cold Case Protection
Cold Case Discovery
Cold Case Murder Mystery

Covert Cowboy Soldiers

The Lost Hart Triplet
Small Town Vanishing
One Night Standoff
Shot in the Dark
Casing the Copycat
Clandestine Baby

Visit the Author Profile page at Harlequin.com.

CAST OF CHARACTERS

Zeke Daniels—Former North Star operative. Decided to buy a ranch and stay in Sunrise, Wyoming, to be near his siblings, but is still trying to figure out what to do with his life.

Brooke Campbell—A forensic anthropologist and was also once a North Star operative. Currently investigating the discovery of multiple skeletal remains in a cave in Bent County, Wyoming.

Carlyle Daniels—Zeke's sister. Living with Cash Hudson.

Walker Daniels—Zeke's brother. Married to Mary Hudson (now Daniels).

The Hudsons—Six brothers and sisters who run a cold case investigative group.

Thomas Hart & Laurel Delaney-Carson—Detectives with Bent County Sheriff's Department who are helping Brooke with the case.

Royal Campbell—Brooke's brother.

Granger Macmillan—Zeke and Brooke's former boss at North Star, along with his wife, Shay.

Chapter One

Brooke Campbell knew she was being followed.

Okay, scratch that. She didn't *know* it. There was no clear, incontrovertible proof. And there were certainly times when she was deep in a case and her paranoia got the best of her.

Maybe she was imagining things. Her current case was deep and disturbing. She'd originally been brought to Sunrise, Wyoming, to study the found human remains of two bodies, but when that assignment had ended with two police officers being held captive in a cave, it had led to the discovery of even *more* remains.

Brooke's latest count was up to twenty different corpses discovered deep in the cave system of a local nature preserve. As a forensic anthropologist, she had excavated and studied many human remains, but never so many in one place.

Brooke loved her work, but some cases were…more affecting. Especially since the police thought they had the perpetrator locked up and… Brooke wasn't so sure.

Still, it was possible the fact that this same silver sedan had been tailing her every day for the past three days was a coincidence.

She really wanted it to be. When she turned into the

parking lot of the little diner, a deviation from the past two days, and the car didn't follow, she breathed a sigh of relief.

Her relief lasted only about ten minutes. She was seated in a booth by the window, sipping her coffee and waiting for her food, when out of the corner of her eye, she saw a familiar silver sedan pull into the parking lot across the way.

It parked. No one got out.

She could keep ignoring it. Pretend it wasn't happening. No one had tried to approach her. There'd been no threat of or attempt at violence toward her, so who knew what it might be about. If it *wasn't* a coincidence, then it might not be nefarious. She likely shouldn't worry about it.

But the last thing she wanted to do was to return to her pretty and cozy and *isolated* rental cabin all by herself for the night knowing that someone *might* be following her. Camped out across the street *watching* her.

She could call the police. She knew quite a few Bent County deputies and detectives now, as well as some deputies and the sheriff from the Sunrise—and her rental cabin was technically *in* Sunrise so these would all be reasonable people to reach out to. But…

If she was going to tell them, she would have done it already. And she *hadn't* told them for a number of reasons. But it came back to a simple one.

She wanted to crack this case. She was so close. It would be the biggest of her career—not just because of the unfathomable body count, but for how long the skeletal remains had been hidden.

Brooke had solved a lot of crimes as a forensic anthropologist, but this one would point to more than just the current suspect. It would, hopefully, allow the police to find another murderer. Worst of all, Brooke still hadn't reached the end of remains—which meant there were more bodies to analyze and hopefully identify. Maybe another person could do it, but she didn't *want* that.

Maybe she wasn't the best forensic anthropologist in the world, but she knew she was good, with a unique set of skills. She couldn't risk being taken off the case.

She was afraid any threat to her—real or only perceived—would have her lifted from it. Granted, isolated Wyoming wasn't thick on the ground with forensic anthropologists, but *still*. She had to protect her ability to keep working.

She sat with that feeling for another ten minutes. Excavating it. Because she did have an alternative to telling the police. But she needed to know, for sure, that she wasn't making excuses so she would *have* to take the alternative.

Zeke Daniels. Oh, he'd been such a mistake. She still couldn't believe she was back in his orbit after all this time, but his friends had needed a forensic anthropologist and he knew one of those.

Or had. Very well. Very, *very* well. Back when they'd both been members of a secret group that had first organized to take down a dangerous and powerful biker gang in South Dakota. After they'd succeeded in that mission, they'd taken on others until the entire organization had disbanded about three years ago.

And in between those two things, she had fallen in love with Zeke Daniels and he'd let her think he'd loved her too. Then he'd broken her heart, crushed it into teeny-tiny pieces. Maybe she'd been naïve enough to deserve it, and maybe it hadn't even been *all* his fault.

Brooke scowled into her coffee. No, she didn't *want* to

see Zeke. Maybe she was curious about how he'd fared, but she didn't want to risk getting caught up in *him* again.

So, she supposed, that was her answer. She didn't *want* his help but kind of needed it.

She pulled out her cell phone, still watching the car across the road through her peripheral vision. She brought up the email he'd last sent her that had included his phone number in case she "needed anything" while in Sunrise. Brooke typed the number into her phone, doing her best to never fully take her gaze off the car.

It rang once, then a deep voice answered.

"Brooke?"

Did he have her number programmed into his phone? *Wow, Brooke, that means absolutely nothing.* Unfortunately the whole *body* reaction to his voice meant more than she'd like.

"Hi, Zeke."

"Everything all right?"

"Of course…not." She certainly wouldn't be calling him if everything was *all right*, and he knew it, even if her first instinct was always to tell everyone she was fine and everything was just great. Luckily, she no longer cared what Zeke thought of her. She didn't care if he thought her request was needy because she didn't *need* him. Or want him.

The end.

"I think I'm being followed." Best to be quick and to the point.

She squinted out the window, to where the silver sedan still sat. She couldn't make out how many people were in it, but she knew no one had gotten out. The license plate was shrouded in shadow and had never been close enough for her to read the letters or numbers, no matter how she'd tried.

There were a few beats of silence. She didn't rush to fill them like she might have once. She'd learned a thing or two about how to use the skills from her job in her personal life. She'd learned a thing or two about *life* since parting ways with one Zeke Daniels.

"Where are you?" he asked.

"The diner." Only one of those around Sunrise.

"Give me about fifteen."

She didn't know exactly what that meant, but the line went dead and she rolled her eyes. He'd never been a man of many words.

Certainly never the ones she'd wanted to hear.

The waitress served her the food she'd ordered and, even though she didn't feel hungry anymore, Brooke forced herself to eat. It was important to keep up her energy and focus for her job, and not let emotions get in the way.

People following her or not, she was going to keep working on this case. She was going to give the detectives every last piece of information she could so they could get to the bottom of it.

So far, she'd unearthed almost twenty skeletal remains in that cave. *Twenty.* And she didn't think she was done. It was a gruesome thought, and gruesome work but it gave people answers. So the nightmares were worth the outcome if she could provide answers.

Her phone trilled. A text from Zeke.

Get up, pretend you're going to the bathroom, then take back exit. Waiting in my truck.

Well, he hadn't gotten any less demanding in the years since she'd last seen him.

Another text came in.

Leave your coat.

Now she scowled at her phone. Typed her own response.

I like my coat.

Leave it so they think you're coming back.

Hard to argue with *that,* she supposed. But she also needed to pay her bill. She could hardly stiff this small-town diner for her meal. Surreptitiously, under the table, she rummaged through her purse until she found a twenty. She slid it under her plate, making sure her arm would hide what she was doing to anyone who might be watching from outside.

Then she got up and made a big show about asking where the restroom was. The woman pointed to the hallway leading to the restrooms…and no doubt the back exit Zeke had spoken of.

Brooke's job was investigation—*old* investigations at that—so she didn't deal with a lot of danger, but she'd seen her fair share as a member of the North Star team.

And before.

But she didn't think about *before* if she could help it. Too many old ghosts, nightmares and regrets.

She walked past the restroom door, through the kitchen, without paying any mind to the speculative look from a dish washer, and then out the back.

Where a large, shiny black truck was parked as close to the door as allowed, its passenger-side door open. Head high, she did her best to crawl up into the seat without looking foolish. She doubted she'd managed. But she settled in the seat and closed the door behind her.

She didn't want to look at him but supposed she had to. She braced herself for impact, plastered a polite smile on her face and turned to face him as he began to drive.

He had not changed. Which was a real bummer. Because Zeke Daniels was ostensibly the most attractive man she'd ever laid eyes on. Worse, he knew it, if he thought about it at all, which was questionable because she figured his thoughts were likely more serious in nature.

He was the tortured-brooding-loner type. And she had, once upon a time, been the kind of silly girl who'd believed she'd get through to that type. Love them into change.

Luckily, she was older and wiser even if he was not any less hot. All dark wild hair and *gigantic* body that made this humongous truck look tailored for a giant of muscle such as he.

It was very, very unfortunate that she could remember just how his muscles had felt under her hands.

"Stay low," was all he said.

Despite her feelings on *him*, she followed instructions, slumping down in the seat so as they drove out onto the road and passed where the silver sedan was parked no one would see her inside.

"I talked to Ida. She called Sunrise SD, saying the car was scaring away customers. Someone will question the driver."

"Oh." Well, that was all good and smart. Not that she knew who Ida was. But Zeke kept driving. Brooke peered at the passing landscape then at him again. His eyes were focused on the road, his square jaw tense—as always—but his hands on the steering wheel looked relaxed enough.

Large hands that have touched every single inch of you.

She tried to ignore the heat that crept into her cheeks—a mix of embarrassment and remembering.

"Where are we going?" she asked.

"My place. You'll be safe there."

Safe? She doubted that.

ZEKE KNEW HE was making a mistake. It wasn't just because Brooke was Brooke, though that was some of it. Part of the mistake was treating this like a North Star mission when his old group of secret special operatives had disbanded, going into civilian work, and leaving him…

At loose ends.

He'd bought a ranch. He still couldn't quite believe it, but since his sister had acted like it was the greatest level of insanity he'd ever stooped to, he'd pretended it had been his plan all along.

He hadn't decided if he liked it or not yet. There was a lot of work to be done to get it back in working order, and he didn't mind the work. He in fact enjoyed work—the harder, the better.

But the chance to jump back into something dangerous…well, that was like coming home. It was familiar. It made him feel…useful.

That was probably not mentally healthy, but a guy couldn't win them all. Besides, Brooke was in his truck looking…like Brooke. Strawberry-blond hair pulled back all sleek and professional, serious blue eyes that should really be *run-of-the-mill* but somehow weren't. Not with her intelligence and warmth behind them. She still had that peaches-and-cream complexion that showed a blush all too well, and he could not go thinking about *that*.

He turned off the highway and onto the bumpy gravel road that led down to his dilapidated ranch house. The drive needed regrading, but that didn't hold a candle to what needed to be done to the house as a whole. He'd made different parts livable—the living room, the kitchen, his bedroom and one upstairs guest room. A work in progress that he'd never once felt even the least bit ashamed of.

Until now.

"Oh, dear." Brooke was looking at the house with a kind of crestfallen expression that made him want to laugh for some inexplicable reason.

"Not quite the accommodations you're used to?"

"It's not about the accommodations, Zeke," she said, affecting that scolding tone that had, once upon a time, made him grin. "It's the fact it's your chosen one."

"I'm renovating." He pushed the truck into Park in front of the house.

She made a considering—and disbelieving—sound.

But she got out of the truck at the same time he did. She walked toward the house, studying the sagging eaves and the one window, currently held together by duct tape, that needed to be replaced. She hesitated a moment before following him up the rickety stairs—he skipped the splintered one.

He unlocked the door and, even though he wasn't watching her, he *was* observing her. Just as he had been since she'd stepped out of the diner.

She wasn't quite the same as the last time they'd seen each other. That made sense. It had been close to four years ago. She had a different kind of…poise now. A stillness that hadn't been in her when she'd been young and... he didn't like the word *desperate*, but there had been a kind of driving need inside her. To be useful, to help, to never be a nuisance or a problem.

So, naturally, he'd taken all that shaky trust she'd had in him and broken it. He didn't like to think he'd been the cause of any change in her, and maybe he hadn't. She'd had four years out in the real world, maybe it had instilled some wariness in her.

Good. He didn't need another chance at shattering the fragile glass she'd once been made of.

When she stepped inside behind him, she made another little noise. A kind of startled *oh* much more positive than the last one.

The note of surprise to her voice made him smile in spite of himself. Because the outside looked pretty awful, but he'd done a hell of a lot of work on parts of the inside. The living room and kitchen weren't half bad—if the duct-taped window was ignored, which he'd fix any day now.

Really.

"Not living in total squalor," he offered, but his phone rang before he could say anything else. He pulled it out of his pocket and took the call from Ida, the lady who ran the diner and kept him fed more nights than not.

He listened grimly then thanked her before relaying the information she'd shared to Brooke.

"The car was gone when the cops got there. Ida said it took off not long after me, though not in the same direction. Not sure I like that." Had they seen her? Or just gotten antsy because she hadn't come back to the table they no doubt had been watching. "Did you get the plate?"

She shook her head. "They didn't have a front plate. I never could get a look at the back."

Zeke nodded. Probably no back plate either if they really were following her. "The crew you're working with at Bent County should know. Is that the detectives?"

She shook her head. "I don't want the detectives to know."

He frowned at her. Surely she'd learned *something* about keeping herself safe after years of investigating dead bodies. "You have a death wish?"

"No," she replied evenly. "I think we discovered long ago that was your problem, not mine."

Oh, so true. Sometimes he thought he'd changed in that regard. Gotten too old or watching his siblings settle down or something. The kind of *something* that had prompted him to buy this ranch when he'd never owned a piece of property in his entire life, never even dreamed about it. But then something like this came along and...

Well, he didn't know what he felt.

"I apologize," Brooke said so formally. "We shouldn't discuss...long ago."

The way she talked, all prim and proper, like she'd been raised in a mansion, gone to some fancy Ivy League school. But no. She'd affected that on her own through grit and determination.

He wished he didn't know it.

"You called me because you're worried. Clearly, I was a last resort."

"Yes, because I don't want the detectives to know. I need to finish this case. It's... I need to. If they're worried about threats to me, I'll either get replaced or they'll worry more about new threats than the very important information I'm *this* close to uncovering."

"I thought they knew who killed those people. What more important information could there be?"

She hesitated, because clearly she knew more about the case than he did and she probably shouldn't be sharing details with just anyone.

But he wasn't *just* anyone.

"If you want me to keep you safe, Brooke, I have to know what I'm keeping you safe from."

Chapter Two

Brooke knew Zeke wasn't *wrong*. You had to know what a threat was to be able to neutralize it, but she just didn't know for sure if it was a real threat. It skirted a very careful line to let a civilian in on a case.

Especially since she hadn't shared her theories with the detectives yet.

Of course, Zeke was hardly a *civilian*. She didn't know how to classify a man who'd been in the army, been a North Star operative taking down gang members and who knew what else, but "civilian" didn't cover it even if he was no longer affiliated with either of those things.

"Brooke. You came to me for a reason, and you knew I'd need to know."

"I didn't think that far ahead, to be honest. I just knew I didn't want to be alone in my rental tonight." Did that sound like an invitation? It was decidedly *not*, and she almost opened her mouth to say so, but reason won out.

He knew what she meant. She didn't need to embarrass herself on top of it.

"Okay, well, think that far ahead now. Explain to me what you're afraid of. You can trust me."

When it came to *personal* matters, she wouldn't trust Zeke Daniels as far as she could throw him. But when it came to this sort of thing? Investigations and danger and searches for the truth?

She could trust him implicitly. It was why she'd called him. Why she'd come here, despite wanting to keep as far away from Zeke as she'd been doing the past month of being in Sunrise. He was right, she *had* to explain it to him.

And still... "Can I have something to drink? Some water, maybe?"

He frowned at the diversion but motioned her to follow him and led her into a pretty little kitchen. The furniture was bachelor terrible, but the cupboards were nice— clearly new and part of his renovation—as were the appliances. And a huge window dominated the wall over the sink and looked out over a beautiful mountain view.

She stood a moment, just taking it in. It needed some lace curtains to flutter in the breeze when the window was open, but other than that, it was absolutely, stunningly, perfect. A cozy kitchen with an awe-inspiring view.

That reminded her this ranch, this house he was renovating, was everything he'd once said he'd never want. Bitterness threatened to rise up, and this wasn't the place for that. Their "back then" didn't matter to the present. She *refused* to be bitter over something long gone. Her own mistake for thinking she could change a man like Zeke.

She took the glass of water he handed her and then took a seat at the small kitchen table when he gestured at the chair. He sat across from her—which might as well be right next to her as small as the table was. As big as *he* was.

Well, at least he hadn't filled this house with a wife and children. That might have actually sent her over the

edge. Not that she knew for *sure* there wasn't a wife wan
dering about, but no signs of a woman or children so—

Put the past aside, Brooke.

She sucked in a breath, carefully let it out. "I've been
excavating the bones in the cave in the preserve for weeks
now, right?" she said, focusing on work, because that
was what she did best. Slowly, carefully, methodically
pick apart the tiniest thing to create a picture, an answer.

He nodded. He had that intense investigator look on.
Paying attention to every word. Filing it away. Like she'd
reversed time and landed them back at North Star.

"There's…a lot. A lot of remains. A lot of *victims*, essentially," she continued. "I know that rumor has made
its way around Bent County, and it's true. It was clearly
some kind of…mass burial. Except, not all done at the
same time. Bodies over the course of years."

"So Jen Rogers killed more than just the Hudson parents?"

Here was where it got tricky. Jen Rogers was the current suspect and had confessed to the murders of the first
two people Brooke had excavated and identified. Because
she'd been living in the cave for a portion of the past few
years, the assumption was the other victims had been
killed and buried by her hand as well.

But Brooke had a different theory. A more complicated one. "Jen Rogers is forty-six years old. Some of the
bones I've found…based on what I've tested, what I've
observed… I think they've been there for closer to fifty
years."

Zeke absorbed that information. Jumped to the conclusion immediately. "There's another murderer? An older
murderer?"

"It's one possibility. It could also be innocuous. Fifty

years is a long time. I haven't been able to study all the bodies, determine causes of death. These could be…accidents or have other reasonable explanations behind them." She tried to tell herself that, but she understood too well what she'd found.

"If it was innocuous, you wouldn't be being followed."

"We don't know for sure that I am, or that it connects." But she was gratified that it was his immediate conclusion as well. Even if she felt honor-bound to argue with him.

An investigator had to look at *every* angle. That, he should know, considering he'd been one in his own right. More than the "shooting the bad guys, running into danger" kind and less of the "sending highly scientific reports to law enforcement agencies" kind.

He clearly didn't agree with her that there might be multiple possible answers here, but it was true. In *her* investigations, she had to weigh every possibility, and there was always the possibility that these older bodies were a coincidence. Something innocent from a long ago time.

"Why haven't you told the detectives?" Zeke asked.

"I'm waiting on test results to ensure my observations are correct, or at least more plausible than not. I can't work on supposition, and neither can the detectives. We need facts. I should have answers in the next few weeks and then…maybe."

He stood, that old energy she remembered—and shouldn't—pumping off him. He'd always been this way. *Vibrant.* It had thrilled her back before it had flattened her. So she'd rebuilt her life around the old tenants that had gotten her into adulthood. Peace, calm, the careful unearthing of teeny-tiny facts that lead to bigger pictures.

Never being too big of a burden. Never hoping for too much from anyone. She was an island, and she had to remember that. She had to remember that no matter what *he* was, she was Brooke Campbell.

"Where do these tests get run?" he demanded.

She didn't like being *interrogated*, but she supposed she only had herself to blame since she'd been the one to contact him. And she knew him. Maybe he'd changed in four years—hence the ranch and the settling down. She'd certainly changed herself. But right now he seemed very much like the Zeke she'd known. No use not answering his demanding questions.

"The state crime lab in Cheyenne."

"That means what you send them passes through a lot of hands."

"It's a murder investigation. Of course it does. I doubt anyone has drawn the conclusions I've drawn yet. But they will if someone's looking to connect things. The detectives will, once they have all the facts."

Zeke paced the kitchen in front of that beautiful window view. A beautiful view in it of himself. Like a predator, sleek and smooth and…

Dangerous, if you recall. But aside from breaking her heart there at the end, he'd always been kind and gentle and—

Don't start that again. She looked down at her hands.

"But if someone knows what's in that cave, they might have cause to follow you. Have cause to see if *you* put what *they* know together."

"Those are all *ifs*."

"Don't be naïve, Brooke."

A sharp order that landed with the pain it had four years ago. For a second, she could only stare at him and wonder if she'd wandered into some kind of time slip because it had landed with so much of that old pain she thought she'd gotten over.

But she didn't have time to deal with that as she heard a door slam open and a woman's voice call out his name.

He muttered an oath under his breath. "Prepare yourself for the onslaught."

IT MIGHT HAVE been funny, the look on Brooke's face as Carlyle whirled through his house, if he didn't think Carlyle had the ability to see right through him when it came to Brooke Campbell.

Too many old ghosts still haunted him when it came to her, and it was not a comfortable realization to find that he liked the look of her at his kitchen table. He had not *once* allowed himself to think of her when he'd bought this ranch, started on renovations.

And now she was just *here,* like that's exactly who he'd been thinking about, and he knew he'd never be able to erase *that.*

His sister stormed into the kitchen—not because something was wrong, no doubt, but because she was just a storm herself.

"What are you doing here?" he demanded.

"Hi to you too," Carlyle replied, already studying Brooke. "You're that forensic person, right?"

Brooke smiled, but Zeke recognized it as the prim, professional one she trotted out when she was uncomfortable.

He didn't like the knowledge he remembered all her different smiles either.

"Brooke Campbell." She held out a hand for Carlyle to shake.

Carlyle slid a glance at him then shook Brooke's hand.

"You knew each other back when he was being Mister Super Secret Spy?"

"Yes."

This was followed by a beat of silence where Carlyle studied Brooke and then him.

"And about as talkative on the matter as you are," Carlyle grumbled.

Even now, with North Star disbanded, it was second nature for him to just not talk about it. North Star had been a *secret* group, and maybe it wasn't so much now, but he still didn't just hand out details.

He'd spent years disbanding a dangerous and vicious gang, another year unraveling other terrifying missions. He'd leapt into danger time and time again, and his sister didn't need the details on that.

Ever.

"Because there's nothing to talk about," Zeke said gruffly. "Brooke, this is my sister. Carlyle."

He couldn't really remember if he'd ever mentioned Car to Brooke back then. North Star had meant keeping family ties close to the vest. It had meant not letting on that you had a real life outside those secret walls. But Zeke had too many memories of telling Brooke way more than he should have.

Brooke smiled politely at Carlyle. "It's nice to meet you. I've heard...things about you."

Carlyle laughed, loud and brash. "I just bet. Well, I need to talk to Zeke for a sec." She studied the woman then turned her gaze on Zeke. "Come to dinner tonight."

He scowled. "I don't want to go to a Hudson dinner." Carlyle and their oldest brother Walker had entangled themselves in the Hudson family, the Hudson Ranch.

Walker marrying and procreating with Mary Hudson—
Daniels now. Carlyle hooking up with Cash Hudson.

All sorts of domestic bliss Zeke preferred to keep his
distance from.

"I didn't ask if you *wanted* to. I told you to come."

"I'm busy." He looked pointedly at Brooke. "Someone's following her."

"Did you go to the cops?" Carlyle asked Brooke.

She shook her head. "It's...complicated."

"Ah, well, maybe *she* should stay with the Hudsons
then. It's got better security than this place. You can both
come for dinner and stay."

The denial was immediately on the tip of his tongue. It
wasn't a *smart* denial, but there and knee-jerk all the same.

Brooke spoke before he could find the right words to
get Carlyle to back off.

"I know what I mean to the Hudsons," Brooke said.

Her voice was cool and calm, but Zeke hated that hint
of vulnerability he could see in her eyes. Because she'd
always been the girl who didn't quite fit in. Things he
never should have let her tell him about herself.

"I don't think I'd be welcome," Brooke said as if it
didn't bother her, but Zeke would lay money on the fact
it did.

"You gave them answers," Carlyle said with about as
much gentleness as his sister gave anyone. "I know you'd
be welcome."

"I examined the skeletal remains of their parents. I'm
sure they're grateful for the positive ID. Sheriff Hudson
has told me as much, but...no one wants to be reminded
of that, and my presence *would* be a reminder. Even if
they were kind enough to not want it to be."

Carlyle was silent a moment then shook her head. "I'm

sorry, you're way too sweet and calm and, like, smart-sounding to stay with this Neanderthal."

It was clearly an attempt to lighten the mood and he knew Brooke was good at that. Going along with the attempts people wanted.

"I don't doubt it. Luckily, I'm not staying with him. I'm just…seeking his counsel on how to proceed."

Zeke's scowl settled deeper. Like hell she wasn't staying with him when she was in *clear* danger. "Yeah, and that *counsel* is going to keep me busy tonight. I'll come up to the ranch some other night." He started ushering Carlyle out of the kitchen, into the living room, *almost* to the front door.

"You messed her up, didn't you?" she asked.

"Goodbye, Car." Before he could effectively usher his sister out of his house, she stopped him with a very simple sentence.

"I think Cash and I are going to get married."

It shouldn't be any kind of shock and yet… "Huh?"

"He asked me to. And I said yes. So, barring end-of-the-world-type stuff brought on by the Daniels clan settling down, I guess it'll happen." She opened the front door herself, stepped out onto the rickety porch. "Anyway, that's what we were going to announce at dinner."

"I'm not settling down." That was perhaps not how he should respond to the news his baby sister was getting married. To a guy he happened to like. But Zeke was who he was.

Carlyle gestured at his house. The one he'd *bought*. He did not allow himself to include Brooke in her gesture. "Sure you're not. Remind me the last time you stayed in one place for more than three months, let alone a year, and—oh, yeah—*bought land*."

"It doesn't mean I'm..." He shook his head. "Congrats, Car. I'm glad. Cash'll keep you in line." He'd only said that to piss her off, because they were who *they* were.

Yet she didn't fume. She didn't even laugh. She studied him with those careful eyes. She didn't trot that out too often, especially now that she wasn't keeping secrets from him and their other brother.

"It doesn't hurt, you know."

"What doesn't?"

"Building something you decide to keep forever."

Since he didn't want to touch *that* with a ten-foot pole, he offered his own version of emotional honesty that would ideally get her running. "They're lucky to have you, Car."

Just as he'd predicted, his sister turned away. "Maybe we're all lucky," she muttered and then strode for her truck where one of her ever-present dogs sat in the passenger side.

She didn't go to the driver's side. She opened the dog's door and shooed it out, then gave it an order to stay.

"I don't need a dog," Zeke said, not quite sure what she was up to as she made her way to the driver's side of the truck.

But she didn't even look at him. She got in her truck, closed the door and leaned out the open window as she backed away.

Carlyle pointed to the house. "She might."

Chapter Three

Brooke was still in the kitchen. She didn't know what to do with the fact she'd just met a member of Zeke's family.

She'd *known* he had siblings. He'd never named them, and hadn't spoken *much* about them, but every once in a while he'd let it slip that he had a brother—older—and a sister—younger. And Brooke had foolishly filed every little detail away and *still* remembered them, apparently.

Now she'd *met* the sister. Carlyle. A pretty, wild thing who didn't look too much like Zeke. Nor did she act like Zeke, who was all still gruffness. Even when she'd seen behind that steely guard of his, there hadn't been a lot of…untamed in Zeke Daniels.

Well…except possibly in one place that it would really not do her to think about at the moment.

She heard a strange noise and looked up to see a large dog trotting inside, Zeke behind it. But she didn't look at Zeke, because the dog came right up to her and pressed its enormous head against her leg, pushing his head under her hand.

Demanding to be petted.

Charmed, and almost immediately in love, Brooke did just that. Slid her hand down its silky head. "Well, hello. What's your name?"

"Consider him your loaner guard dog."

Brooke blinked at Zeke. She'd figured this was his dog. "What?"

"Carlyle and her... Well, you've met Cash Hudson. They train dogs together. She left this one for you."

"My rental doesn't allow pets."

"Guess you'll have to stay here then."

She sighed, trying not to let the frustration win. She had to be reasonable. "Zeke, I'm not staying here."

"You were scared. You called me because you're scared."

"Yes, but..." What was the *but*? She didn't know. She just...had made a mistake, clearly. Letting fear and instinct lead her to the wrong decision. Because she should have known, even with the past firmly in the past, he would take over. He would be high-handed and too...*him*.

"So, it's me and the dog protecting you and you stay here, or we tell the detectives. Your job or your pride. I'll let you pick."

Had he always been so unreasonable?

Yes.

She kept petting the dog in an effort to keep herself calm. It didn't work. "I'm not your responsibility, and in fact, when I was even a little bit of your responsibility, you didn't handle that very well."

His expression didn't change. Because he was expressionless. Blank. Yes, she remembered that quite well—especially at the end.

"No, I didn't."

That admission felt...heavy. Shifted too many things inside her, made her heart pick up a little. Especially the way he just *looked* at her, those serious, intent dark eyes. Four years and the way it had ended should have dulled whatever impact those eyes could have.

But they didn't. She felt too warm and could remember all too well the way…

No, Brooke, you are not letting yourself remember that.

"How about this? We'll sit down. Eat a little dinner. You make a list of people who might have some inclination of where you're leaning with your findings. Then I'll work on finding out if any of them have a silver sedan that matches the one following you."

"And what will I do while you work on that?"

"Whatever you need to. You have your computer in that giant purse, right?"

She wrinkled her nose and held it a little closer. "Yes."

"So, work. That's what you'd be doing back at your rental, isn't it?"

She hated that he knew that about her. Even if it was just an educated guess.

"Sit. Make a list." He rummaged through a drawer and then handed her a pen and a pad of paper. "I'll put together something for us to eat."

He used to do that. He wasn't as good a cook as she was, but he was adept enough in the kitchen. He'd always been closed-lipped about his background, but as they'd gotten closer, things had slipped out.

Abusive father. Moved a lot. Mother murdered. She didn't know at exactly what age he'd been when that had happened, but she knew he'd been a teenager and had only been kept on the straight and narrow—ish—by his older brother. Then Zeke had enlisted the moment he'd been able. He'd done a stint in the army for a few years before he'd moved over to North Star.

Did he remember the things about *her* past that she'd told him? Things she'd never told anyone outside of the people who'd known against her will.

It all made her feel tired and sad, so she sat at his kitchen table and focused on petting the dog. "What's his name?"

"*Her* name. Viola."

She smiled at the dog's warm brown eyes. "Viola. Named after a pretty flower, and you're a pretty thing, aren't you?" she cooed at the dog. Then worked on her list while Zeke did the domestic work of throwing together a meal.

He put a bowl of pasta in front of her after a while and then plopped a plastic canister of Parmesan cheese next to her. "And before you say it, I know the fresh stuff is better, but this keeps longer so it wins for a single guy."

Their gazes caught across the table.

He'd just made it clear he remembered her pasta cheese preferences, all these years later. And her foolish heart fluttered at the thought. Just as bad, he'd also made it clear he was single. Like that was *relevant*, when it was decidedly not.

She looked down at the list she'd made. Slid it over the table to him. "It's short."

"Then it'll be quick and easy."

He looked over it then crossed off the first person on the list. "I know Hart doesn't have a silver sedan."

Detective Thomas Hart was the lead detective on the case, along with his partner, Laurel Delaney-Carson. Brooke liked them both, and knew they weren't the ones behind whoever was following her, but she didn't say that. She let Zeke draw his own conclusions.

"In the morning, I'll take you to your car. You can do everything you normally do in a day. I'll just be… watching. See if we can find that sedan, get a plate, an ID on the driver."

She frowned at that. "What are you going to do? Pull them over?"

"No. We'll play it by ear."

She rolled her eyes. *We*, her butt. Much as she hated to admit it though, she felt more at ease here than she had at the diner or her rental. She could have all sorts of issues with Zeke's heavy-handed overbearing *male* nonsense, and her reaction to Zeke as a *man* she'd once known intimately, but she knew he'd keep her safe. Regardless of how he felt about her. Or how she felt about him.

She sighed and then, when they were done eating, she cleaned up. An old habit from living in the same North Star places. Because those who cooked, didn't clean and vice versa.

"I'll show you your room," he said once they were finished.

An awkward silence settled over them. She nodded, grabbed her tote bag and followed him up stairs that had clearly been recently fixed. The hallway was a bit of a disaster, but he led her to a pretty room. Sparse, certainly. It could do with some…softer touches, but the bed looked big and comfortable, and the window gave the same view as the one down in the kitchen.

"Just one night," she said firmly. Because she was determined. *Determined*. She could butt heads with him and win. She would. And she could do it on her own. After they figured out the silver sedan.

She turned to face him in the doorway, ignored the way his gaze still hit her bloodstream like heat and want. But she did not want him.

She would not.

"Good night, Zeke."

"Night, Brooke," he returned. But he didn't move to walk away.

So she closed the door carefully in his face. Because she was *not* going down that old road ever again.

If she knew even in her head it sounded like she was protesting way too much, she ignored it.

ZEKE TOOK THE dog out for one last bathroom run once he was sure Brooke was settled in her room. He didn't worry that she'd run—that wasn't Brooke. What he did worry about was…everything else.

Someone being after her.

Her being in his house looking the same as she had four years ago when he'd realized he'd needed to purposefully end things before he accidentally hurt her was…

Well, it messed with his head was what it did. Because he didn't like people in his space. Didn't even like Walker and Mary coming over with their baby. Or Carlyle and Cash coming over with Izzy, Cash's thirteen-year-old. Or, the worst, *all* of them coming over and acting like a big happy family.

It felt too much like some old dream of a future he'd never really believed in. Functional relationships and people who were good parents to their kids. Family. Walker and Carlyle had somehow found themselves those sitcom happy endings—not without some pain and danger along the way—but they'd gotten it all the same.

Zeke didn't really know what was worse. Thinking he didn't get to have it, or thinking he was lucky to be part of it regardless of his romantic status.

But he did know what was worse in *this* moment. Brooke in his house, and the feeling she was what had always been missing. Her smile and blue eyes and floral scent.

When *that* was ridiculous. Maybe he'd loved her way back then, not that he'd have ever admitted it to himself or to her in the moment. Sure, maybe looking back now, he could admit it.

But he'd loved his plans, his revenge, his danger more.

And now you don't have any of those things.

Yeah, it didn't do to think about that at all. He should think about her case. Her safety.

It seemed whoever was behind those bones didn't like anyone snooping around in them. That meant *anyone* could be following her. Her sending things off to a lab in Cheyenne had left a lot of things open for leaks, for coming back to hurt her.

She needed her own lab. She couldn't trust the bureaucracy of government officials. Hell, that was the whole reason North Star existed.

Had existed. He didn't know how many years it would take him to accept that they were really done. Retired. He'd had enough of his own personal danger since then not to dwell much on it.

Until the past few months.

Now he had a new purpose. Because maybe Brooke Campbell couldn't ever mean anything to him, but he wasn't about to let anything happen to her.

He watched the dog frolic in the yard under a moonlit sky. After a while, he pulled his phone out of his pocket. He dialed an old number.

"Zeke, if you're calling to drag me into another dangerous mission, count me out. We've got a new foster kid, and Shay somehow corralled me into keeping *chickens*."

Zeke smiled in spite of himself here alone in the dark.

"Nothing dangerous. Nothing that requires your time," he said to his old boss. It was hard to imagine the tough and certain Granger MacMillan, once the head of North Star—the secretive group that had eradicated the Sons of the Badlands gang from everywhere they'd had power—cavorting with chickens and a bunch of foster kids out on his ranch in Montana, with his equally tough and perhaps even scarier wife.

But that's what the end of North Star had given Granger and Shay. Love and family. Just like Zeke's siblings had found.

He didn't like to dwell on it.

"Well, I know you didn't call to have a heart-to-heart," Granger replied.

Zeke snorted. "No. Just a question. What would I need to set up a makeshift forensic lab on my property?"

Granger was quiet for a minute before making a contemplative noise. "I can send you some things. Might take a few days, but I've still got all the old connections."

"That'd be great. Thanks."

"Say hi to Brooke for me," Granger said then laughed. Far too hard. Far too long.

Zeke clicked End on his phone.

But Granger's laughter seemed to echo in his head for a long time after.

Chapter Four

Brooke had slept, and when she woke up blinking at a bright sunny morning outside the window, with that gorgeous view right *there*, she didn't quite know how to get her bearings.

She sat up, scratched her hands through her tangled hair and blew out a breath.

It was perfectly normal to sleep well when you knew you were safe, and she hadn't felt safe in quite some time.

And it wasn't silly or foolish to feel safe in Zeke's house. He was a former soldier, a former North Star agent, and while things hadn't exactly ended well between them, it wasn't because he'd been a *bad* guy. He'd been, and was, in fact, incredibly honorable. And he'd been upfront and honest about all he couldn't give her.

She could be hurt about that and still know that she was in perfectly good hands when it came to him helping to keep her safe from a potential threat.

So, no reason to sit here in this nice bed, brooding over the fact her ex-boyfriend made her feel safe and how much she liked his house.

She sucked in another slow breath. Let it out. She went through the rest of her slow-breathing morning ritual. She even managed a few yoga poses in the small room while the sun gilded the mountains outside.

Sunrise, Wyoming, and the surrounding Bent County was a pretty place to be even if the work that had brought her here was gruesome. It was a *grounding* kind of pretty and awe-inspiring, really. Man's capacity for evil could be soul-crushing. The world's capacity for beauty and miracles was the only antidote she'd ever found for that.

She hadn't brought anything to Zeke's house besides her work bag, so she had to get dressed in her clothes from yesterday. She used her fingers as a comb and tried to tame her wild bedhead back into the clip that had luckily been in her bag.

Once satisfied, she left her room, only to be greeted by the dog from yesterday, lying there in the hall.

"Good morning," she murmured to Viola, who thumped her tail and looked up at Brooke adoringly. As much as she dreaded facing Zeke, the dog's greeting made her smile. "Come on then," she said, gesturing for the dog to follow her downstairs.

She could hear the faint noise of movement in the kitchen, and the smell of coffee hit her once she made it to the bottom of the stairs. She paused a second, did a little more deep breathing while Viola waited at her feet with a seemingly quizzical look on her doggie face.

Brooke put on a polite smile, aimed it at the dog, and was determined she'd aim it at Zeke too. But when she stepped to the threshold of the kitchen, he stood at the stove, cooking eggs in a skillet.

He wore a T-shirt that was old, faded. And perfectly outlined the impressive structure of his *very* muscular body that had not lost any of its strength even though his operative days were over. Almost as bad, he wore loose sweats low on his hips and his feet were bare.

Like every ridiculous domestic fantasy she'd ever had about him all those years ago. Futures and forevers and *family*, when she'd always known those things were not in the cards for her. It was hardly his fault she'd fooled herself into thinking they could be.

Had she made a noise? An embarrassing kind of hum or sigh, or both? Probably.

He glanced over to her and he didn't *quite* smirk, but there was a knowing kind of glint to his eyes that just…

She could *not* do this. She had to go back to her rental tonight. No matter what he said, no matter what happened. She would not survive being in his orbit without embarrassing herself all over again. He was just *too much*. And it didn't matter if that was unfair, because it just was.

She'd stood on her own two feet for most of her life. She'd learned, time and time again, it was the only thing to do. Keep to herself. Rely on herself. And only herself.

"Made some breakfast," he offered. He nodded toward the table. "Have a seat."

She might have argued that she didn't need to be fed and that she didn't have any plans to listen to his orders, but in this moment of jittery heart and some very unwanted *lust*, she decided it best not to speak and to just do as she was told.

So Brooke sat at the table as Viola arranged herself at her feet and Zeke put a plate and mug in front of her. She stared at the contents and did not pay any mind that it was filled with things she liked. Everyone liked toast with butter. Everyone liked scrambled eggs with cheese. And it was hardly any great leap to put the exact right amount of cream in her coffee when she knew he took it the same way. He hadn't *remembered* what she liked.

This was all a coincidence.

But then he slid into the other seat at the table, and his eggs didn't have cheese and his toast had jelly on it.

Her inhale was shaky at best, but she studied her eggs rather than look to see if he was looking at her. The bottom line was, it didn't matter what he thought or felt about her. What he might remember or not. She knew it wasn't that he'd hated her or been disgusted by her or anything. They'd had a very serious relationship for a handful of wonderful months four years ago. It had come to an end because they hadn't wanted the same things out of life.

Maybe it had crushed her, but it wasn't…horrible. He wasn't horrible and she wasn't horrible and…

She really had to get off this roller coaster she'd created. She shoved a bite of eggs into her mouth and they ate in silence for a few minutes. Uncomfortable silence to *her*, but she'd learned that what she felt didn't always translate to Zeke.

"So, what's the plan for today?" she asked, frustrated she had to clear her throat to speak.

"I'll take you to your car after you eat. From there, you can go about your day however you like. I'll be keeping an eye out and doing some investigating of my own."

She finished her toast, pondered how much she was going to allow. Because she should allow *someone* to watch out for her. Better safe than sorry, she kept telling herself.

The problem was, Zeke was a different kind of danger. Maybe she *should* tell the detectives everything and then she wouldn't have to worry about her reaction to him.

But she thought about being taken off this case. Thought

about how many times she'd let things beyond her control rule her life.

She had to be stronger than her feelings.

"And how will you be doing that?" she asked, trying to focus on the task at hand, which was *not* her reaction to Zeke.

"Chasing down this silver sedan, for starters. Don't worry, I'll stay out of your hair. Then we'll meet for dinner at the diner. Compare stories, go from there."

This would not be the first time they'd done that. Him watching out for her. Them comparing stories. That's what had led to their relationship in the first place. She'd been his North Star assignment when one of her investigations into some remains had led to threats against her.

But North Star didn't exist anymore. And neither did they.

"This isn't a North Star mission, Zeke."

He didn't say anything for a long, humming moment. A moment in which he looked almost…lost. That was ridiculous, of course. She wasn't sure Zeke Daniels had been *lost* a second in all his life.

Yet, without North Star… She shook away the thought. How he was faring without his favorite coping mechanism was *none* of her business, and she could not let her mind—or worse, her heart—go back to a place where she believed it was.

"Well, I have to get to the caves," she said, pushing back from the table. "We should get going."

ZEKE HADN'T SAID anything else. He'd simply gotten ready, walked with her and Viola to his truck, and then driven into Sunrise to the diner and her car.

If what she said echoed around in his head like an earworm, it wasn't the first time. Lots of people had pointed out to him that he wasn't an operative anymore, that North Star didn't exist, that everything he'd busted his ass for was just *gone*.

All because *some* people had wanted to start "lives." Why were spouses and babies the be-all and end-all for people? He much preferred living his life on the edge of danger. Solving problems. Uncovering mysteries and stopping bad people from doing terrible things.

The same speech he'd been giving himself for years was getting old, even in the quiet of his own mind.

He pulled his truck into the tiny parking lot of the diner. The morning crowd was dwindling— old ranchers got out and back home early, he'd learned—but a few cars still remained in the lot besides Brooke's. Not a silver sedan among them.

He studied the surroundings, brooding over the situation. Too vague, not enough details, just Brooke's feeling that someone was following her.

But one thing he knew about Brooke was that she didn't jump to conclusions, particularly when it came to her own safety. She was under the impression she could fade into the background if she wanted, that no one paid her much mind.

He snuck a glance at her. She appeared serene, but he saw the way she clutched her hands together in her lap. How stiff and straight her posture was. How *carefully* she breathed.

If he thought too much about it, he'd be reminded of how *haunted* he'd been by not waking up beside her after he'd broken things off. How every morning of not hearing those weird deep breathing things she did had sent him into the strangest kind of pain he'd ever experienced. So confusing and all-encompassing that he'd thrown himself into the most dangerous missions he could a few days later.

Over and over again, until North Star was done. Then he'd thrown himself into finding his mother's murderer— which had been complicated and dangerous enough that Brooke had been easy to keep—mostly—off his mind.

Four years was a long time. He'd figured it was long enough for all *this* not to matter.

Well, he'd been wrong before and would likely be wrong again. Didn't matter. He had to figure out how to *deal*. And, above all else, keep her safe.

She got out of the truck and Viola hopped out after her. Brooke turned, concern on her face as she held the passenger door open. "Zeke, I can't take her around with me. Not to work. Not to my rental."

He wished she could, but understood. Besides, Brooke wasn't staying in that rental tonight no matter what she thought. And if she insisted on staying there against all reason, he and Viola would just camp out right outside. "It's okay. I'll keep her with me."

Brooke looked at him slightly askance, like he was full of it, but she didn't mount an argument. She closed the door and he got out on his side. She was already striding for her car, telling the dog in low tones that she'd have to stay behind.

She reached for her driver's-side door.

"Wait," he ordered. *Not a North Star mission, remember?* He scowled. Maybe it wasn't, and maybe it shouldn't be, but he was still going to do what it took to keep her safe.

He inspected her car, ignoring the imperious way she watched him, and when he found it, was rattled at how close he had been to missing it. But at the last second, he felt the ridge of something that shouldn't be there, right under the back door.

Carefully, without damaging the small disk, he removed the piece. He held it up. Studied it in the light. "Tracker." He took a page out of her book and blew out a slow breath, trying to think through the bright, violent haze of fury. Someone was *tracking* her.

He should have seen that coming. He should have known skeletal remains, even if the supposed perpetrator was behind bars, would bring nothing but trouble.

He'd made the call to bring her in. *He'd* made the decision to be hands off and let the Bent County Sheriff's Department handle it from there.

And *he'd* put her in danger by doing so.

It *burned*.

He looked at her, hoping the leaping fury didn't show in his expression. But she didn't look at him. She stared at the tracker in his hand.

"Oh," was all she said. "That's...not good."

She was going to give him an *aneurism*. Not good? Christ. Without a word, he walked over to his truck and fastened the tracker to the bed.

"What are you doing?" Brooke demanded, her voice high-pitched, her expression angry. He didn't know which part made her angry—the tracker's existence or him putting it on his truck.

It didn't matter. One had already happened and she wasn't about to change his mind on the other.

"They want to track something, they can track me."

"Zeke," she said in that soft way that had fooled him into thinking he could have something soft all those years ago.

He'd learned from that. Besides, after all this time, she

wasn't worried about *him*. She was just worried in that way she had. She didn't ever want anyone going through any trouble for her. Even when she should.

"I can take care of myself, Brooke."

She nodded. "Yes, you always thought so."

Ouch. He brought a hand to his heart with half a thought to rub the pain there away. But she was watching him intently, so he stood still and motionless.

"Can I go now?" she asked archly.

He gestured her along. "Have at it." But he watched her as she gave Viola a pat and quietly apologized to the *dog* that she wasn't allowed to come with her. Once Brooke was in her car, he whistled and Viola reluctantly padded back over to him.

Brooke drove away, and he didn't bother to hide his scowl. He gave one last scan of the parking lot, the diner, the road. Then got back in his truck, Viola in tow, and set about following her himself.

So no one else did.

Chapter Five

Brooke hated being distracted at work. It was rare she couldn't turn off her thoughts and focus on the task at hand—she'd always been good at losing herself in *something* to avoid her unpleasant reality.

It should have been easy. It wasn't like she was alone in the cave. There was always a deputy or detective stationed with her, so she didn't have to worry about her surroundings or being interrupted. She showed up, set out her tools, and got to work. They handled everything else until it was time for a break or time to quit.

Today, she couldn't seem to turn off the outside. The tracker Zeke had found had shaken her up, and maybe she could have set that aside, but thoughts of the device meant also thoughts of Zeke.

She rolled her eyes. To be unsettled by a *man* as a *threat* was ridiculous and made her ashamed. She needed a new approach. Instead of denial, maybe she needed to try acceptance.

Zeke would be a problem until this was done, and she had a lot of work to do. Apparently, she couldn't just ignore her reaction to him, even for a few hours.

But then, what *was* she supposed to do about him?

She rolled her shoulders and refocused on her current task.

She had battery-powered mobile lights set up carefully around the area she worked on. Luckily, she wasn't bothered by enclosed spaces, because this was tight and dark and damp. Not the best conditions for any kind of anthropology, particularly forensic. It made the work challenging. Just the way she liked it.

She took pictures of the new segment she'd just moved to, documenting everything within an inch of its life. If she was right, and these bones were older—too old to be murders perpetrated by the current suspect—there was absolutely no room for error.

Certainly no room to be distracted by *exes*. Even if he was her one and only ex.

The more she excavated in the cave, the more space to bring in more and better light. And she'd certainly done her fair share of work so far. It was alarming and depressing how much work was left to do. Not because she minded the work, but because someone had used this place as their own personal body dumping grounds. But not just *dumping*. People had been carefully buried in secret here.

Brooke set the camera aside, got some tools to start excavating the next square. She crouched and started to work but noticed something kind of odd next to her foot.

She turned her head, so the lamp on her helmet focused in on it. Not bone. Not cave. It could be animal, but... She leaned in closer. It looked an awful lot like the corner of a book.

She reached out and touched it. Felt like a book too. It was shoved in between two rock formations. She was about to pull it out, but looked down and saw how dirty her gloves were. Not a problem with bones and remains buried deep in the cave floor, but paper...

It clearly hadn't been there long because paper would have a lot more damage if it had been left there for *years*. Maybe it would be some kind of clue to incriminate Jen Rogers.

Or whoever else was killing people and burying them down here.

"Thomas?" She was on a first-name basis with the detectives now that she'd spent so much time with them, and Thomas Hart happened to be her partner today. "Do you have a fresh set of gloves?" Hers were by her equipment and she wanted to retrieve this book as carefully and quickly as possible.

"Sure." He held them out to her and she took them. She switched her gloves. Then, with caution, she pulled the book from the crevice it had been shoved into without tearing anything or dragging it in the wet sediment of the ground more than necessary.

Once freed, she looked at it, opened the cover. "It's... a scrapbook."

Thomas was by her side so fast that Brooke almost bobbled the book. Like the word *scrapbook* had jolted through him.

"Not just any scrapbook," he said, looking down over her shoulder. "I think that's the scrapbook that was stolen from the police department last month when we first discovered the remains on the Brink property."

Last month. She could tell this meant a lot to the detective, but it didn't really mean anything to *her* investigation if it didn't involve the potential for a second murderer... even if she *was* curious.

"I don't have anything to pack up this kind of material carefully, but we need to be very gentle. If it's been down here for a whole month in these kinds of conditions, that isn't good for any of the material in a scrapbook. We should get it out of here and consult an archivist. Someone who would know how best to handle it, if it's as old as it looks, and make sure we're preserving it correctly."

Hart looked at her with a slight frown. "Good point." Then he hesitated. Thomas was usually calm, but she could *feel* the tension the scrapbook brought out in him. It was part of his investigation and he wanted to look at it now rather than later.

"If you put some gloves on, you can take it back to the station right now. I'm fine on my own here for a bit."

He shook his head. "Brooke, I wouldn't leave *anyone* in a mass grave all by themselves, even if studying mass graves *is* your job."

Well, mass graves hadn't been her job before. This was a first. But she could detect the impatience waving off him and didn't like to let other people's uncomfortable feelings to *linger*. She'd learned a long time ago to make certain she wasn't a burden to anyone else. A problem.

Life worked better that way.

"Why don't we break for lunch? You can go back to the station and get that squared away, and I'll grab something to eat and meet you there when I'm done."

He smiled at her. "I appreciate it. Want to leave this all set up? I'll have one of the guys park here while we're gone."

Brooke looked around. She'd had a solid two hours of work, but she was definitely in the middle of things. Still, it would be good to take a break, get her head on straight.

She grabbed a few of the evidence bags and boxes she'd filled. "That'll be fine. I'll send these back to the lab while we're at it." It was still work, and maybe some fresh air would help her refocus.

They worked in a comfortable quiet to turn off the lights and then take what she needed out into the bright light of day. Hart was definitely distracted by the discovery of the scrapbook, and Brooke was well aware the *whole* case wasn't her business. Her business was to uncover the remains, study them, test them, identify and form conclusions about them.

Still…

"This scrapbook… It belonged to Jen Rogers?"

Thomas shook his head as she carefully placed the book in his patrol car. "No. It's kind of a long story. You know Chloe Brink, right?"

Chloe was a police officer, and it had been on her and her brother's property the first skeletal remains had been found. Brooke had met her a few times, since she was involved with the Hudsons. "Yes."

"It was a Brink family scrapbook, discovered by Chloe while we were investigating the first two bodies. She brought it in to us, and then…" He trailed off, as if searching for the right words. "Well, I had it. It was stolen from me when…"

Brooke had been around enough to know the story. Feigning a call for help, Jen Rogers and the women who'd been working with her had knocked Thomas unconscious and then dropped him in the middle of the forest preserve where the cave was located. It was why he still had a faint pink scar from the stitches he'd had to get along the side of his face.

"When they took me…" he finally said, clearly still not over *that*. "It was all a ruse to get their hands on this scrapbook. We never could figure out why. Particularly since Jen was only connected to the Brink family through marriage and it was a Brink family scrapbook. But we'll look through it again with what we know, and we'll consult Chloe and see if we can find some answers. Hopefully implicate Jen even more."

No doubt it would, if it was in the cave. But Brooke couldn't help but wonder if it might connect to what else she was thinking. She'd need a look at the scrapbook though. "If she doesn't have any clear-cut answers, would I be able to take a look through it?"

Thomas raised an eyebrow at her. "Why?"

Brooke shrugged. "I don't know exactly. It's just…it has to connect some way, right? To those remains, if she stole it during the investigation into the Hudson murder. Maybe something would…jump out to me as a connection."

Thomas seemed to give this some thought. "Possibly. I'll run it by Laurel, and Chloe, for that matter."

"Sure," Brooke agreed, fully believing she'd *never* see the inside of that scrapbook. But she couldn't focus on that because a trickle of unease crept up her spine, tightening her shoulders. She looked around the bright daylight as Thomas got in his patrol car.

"You okay?" he asked.

Brooke nodded, forced herself to look away from the scenery and to Hart. "Of course. I'll meet you at the station once I've eaten."

"Sounds good." He closed his door, but she knew he'd wait for her to get into her car and drive out first. He'd follow her to the highway. And then he'd go his own way and she would go hers, because he didn't know someone *might* be following her.

But Zeke did, and she would just have to trust that he would take care of it.

ZEKE APPRECIATED THAT it was Hart with Brooke today. He knew a few of the deputies at Bent County, and for the most part he trusted Bent to do their job, but over the past few months he'd actually become friends with Thomas Hart. He'd do a good job looking after Brooke.

She'd definitely sensed Zeke watching her, though he'd stayed out of sight. He didn't know if that's because her instincts were that good, or because he was losing his touch. He didn't love the thought he was rusty, but he *was* getting older. He'd been out of the following game for a while now, so his skills could have deteriorated.

On top of that, he wasn't sure what to make of their early break for lunch. Brooke had only been in there working for about two hours.

It didn't really matter, he supposed. No matter what she did, he was going to be there.

Zeke followed her throughout the rest of her day, and not once did he see any sign of a silver sedan. Following her *or* him in his truck with the tracker now attached.

He wasn't sure what to do with that. Did they know someone had moved their tracker? Had they given up because she'd stayed with him last night?

Were they better stalkers than he was?

That was a concerning question. Not one he'd let rattle him though. He'd find a way to protect Brooke no matter what. And she clearly needed protecting from something if someone was trying to track her—regardless of the whys.

Track, follow, but not approach. Not threaten. He didn't know why, but that made him far more uncomfortable than a direct threat. He knew what to do with threats— stop them in their tracks.

What did whoever was following her *want* from her if

there was no threat? Without motivation, it was going to be harder to get to the bottom of who.

But not impossible, Zeke assured himself as he stood next to his truck in the Bent County Sheriff's Department parking lot, waiting for Brooke to appear after she'd gone inside with Hart at the end of their afternoon shift at the cave.

He didn't know what her plans were, but he knew that the tracker had to have changed things for her. She had to understand even more fully just how much potential danger she was in.

Viola gave a soft whimper from her spot in the passenger seat, head leaning out the window. Zeke watched as Brooke and Hart walked out of the station, practically shoulder to shoulder. Brooke was smiling, and she said something that had Hart doing the same.

A surprisingly sharp bolt of jealousy landed hard, right at the center of Zeke's chest. He didn't want it, knew he had absolutely no right to it, and still it settled there like an intense, squeezing pain.

Brooke stopped in her tracks when she saw him standing there in between her car and his truck.

Hart's eyebrows rose, but he didn't stop walking, so when Brooke finally moved forward again, she had to walk quickly to catch up to the detective.

"Zeke," Hart greeted. His expression was *way* too close to amused. "Needing a detective?"

"No," Zeke returned. And refused to explain himself, even if Hart *was* a friend. Even if there was no reason to feel…competitive.

Hart gave the dog a pet then turned to Brooke with another *smile*. "See you tomorrow, Brooke."

"Bye, Thomas." Her smile faded as she turned her attention to him. "Zeke, you didn't need to be here."

"And yet here I am."

She sucked in a slow breath, and he *refused* to let her annoyance with him and her smiles at Thomas stir up his temper.

"No one's been following me today and you removed that tracker, so they can't again. I think it's best if we go back to the way things were before. If I have concerns... I'll let you know." She moved over to where Viola whimpered in the passenger seat and gave her a rubdown, whispering assuring words to the dog.

But Brooke was *wrong*. Someone had been following her today. The fact that it was *him* was neither here nor there. "Did it occur to you that no one's been following you today because you involved me?"

She gave him a cool look. "Do you think your North Star reputation matters to anyone around here?"

He shrugged. "I'm a physically intimidating guy, Brooke. I don't need a reputation to precede me."

She rolled her eyes and he couldn't help but smile. Because a little spot of color showed up on her cheeks. Like she was considering anything *physical* about him. Or maybe that was just wishful thinking.

Didn't matter.

"Besides, trackers are easy and inconspicuous," he continued. "Someone could drop another one at any time."

She stiffened at that. Maybe four years changed a person, but Zeke knew Brooke well enough to know her refusal wasn't some misplaced bravado. It wasn't that she *wasn't* scared or didn't have concerns. She just never wanted to be seen as a burden by anyone. Back then, she'd always been so scared that...whatever support she got was fleeting. That she needed to handle everything on her own or people would simply…kick her to the curb.

It was one of the few things he didn't think she had any self-awareness about. She thought she was being independent, but what she really was, and always had been, was afraid to be a bother.

He understood, too well, where it stemmed from. Not just her awful childhood stuck in the middle of a Sons of the Badlands family, but then as a foster kid getting kicked around the system.

Knowing all that about her made him softer than he should allow himself to be when it came to her safety.

"If you really want to stay at your rental, I can drop Viola off at the Hudsons' and crash on the couch or something. I can even sleep in the truck outside, if that bothers you."

Her face took on a pinched look, but she continued to speak in that careful, detached kind of way. "That's not the kind of alternative I'm looking for. Thank you."

He *almost* smiled at the tacked-on "thank you," but this was too important to be amused by her. "It's the only one you're going to get, Brooke."

Temper flashed in her blue eyes. "I didn't tell you about this just so you'd swoop in and take over."

"Didn't you?"

Her mouth dropped open—not quite outrage. She wasn't mean enough for outrage. Because something like *hurt* tinged in her expression and it made him feel about two inches tall. Enough that he had to fight the urge to reach forward by shoving his hands into his pockets. Enough that he gentled his words.

"Brooke. You're possibly in some kind of danger. There's no point in being stubborn about wanting and taking some protection. It's not offered out of anything other than concern, so you shouldn't feel badly about taking it."

She inhaled. That slow, careful inhale that signaled she was trying so hard to be *reasonable*.

"You're right," she agreed, somewhat surprisingly. She met his gaze with a cool, determined look. "We'll discuss a fee."

He frowned at her, not following. "A fee?"

"Like hiring a bodyguard. I'll pay you a fee."

He could not think of anything she might have said that could be any more insulting. "You're not going to pay me," he growled.

"Why not? You're offering a service, are you not?"

"Brooke."

"Zeke."

Maybe he'd forgotten *some* things about her because he surely didn't remember this stubbornness of hers ever being directed at him. And it poked at an already frayed temper—not because of her, but because of everything confusing and challenging about this situation.

His feelings chief among them.

"I'm going to be there," he told her. Maybe a little *too* firmly, *too* seriously, too *close*. "Until we get to the bottom of this, or until the job is done. And I'm not taking a dime. The end."

She looked up at him, blue eyes flashing and narrowing with her own temper. Close enough he could see the faint scar on her cheekbone that she used to try to hide with makeup. The one he knew her father had given her the night Family Services had finally intervened and she'd been taken away.

She'd told him that one day all those years ago, before he'd been assigned to protect her but after he'd met her.

He'd teasingly asked about it, trying to flirt with the pretty woman working for Granger MacMillan. Because as seriously as he'd taken his place at North Star, he hadn't been able to stop thinking about her after that first meeting.

She'd recited the facts like they were rote historical events that didn't concern her, and he'd been…even more fascinated. Because he didn't know how someone so fresh and pretty, so gentle and soft seeming, could have come from as terrible a childhood as he had.

And that was before he'd known hers had been worse.

But this was now. He could tell by the anger in her eyes—because she used to not get angry at him. Just hurt by him. He could tell by the fact she didn't respond to him in any way. At least, any *verbal* way.

She whirled around, started striding to her car, even as Viola whined.

Fine. She could get in that car and drive away, but he would follow. He hadn't been exaggerating when he'd said he was in this until the job was done. She didn't need to like it and he didn't need her permission to keep her safe.

She stopped abruptly. She didn't turn to face him, just stood there with ramrod-straight posture. When she spoke, it was quietly but with enough force he could hear.

"I *have* survived a clear, everyday threat. I grew up surviving that."

"I know." And wished he didn't. Because back then he'd really liked thinking no one could have experienced the childhood trauma he'd had. Abusive dad who'd eventually disappeared. Mother murdered in their apartment. A murder it had taken over a decade of danger and pain and frustration to solve. He'd had his share of sorrow and horrible things.

And she'd been raised by a violent psychopath in some

kind of biker cult, and then somehow dealt with the fragile, uneasy life of a teenager in foster care.

But she hadn't let any of her circumstances harden her. Sure, they'd messed her up. They all had scars left from what they'd grown up with—no one who got themselves mixed up with North Star didn't—but she was one of the few he knew who was somehow still…*soft*.

Strong as hell, but penetrable.

Maybe it was wrong, pointless, not his place, or misguided. He didn't care. In this moment, he'd been the one to bring her here. Walker's brother-in-law had needed a forensic anthropologist and Zeke had known one. He'd pulled the strings. *He* was why Brooke was here.

He couldn't and *wouldn't* let anything hit that soft target.

"You shouldn't have had to survive that childhood alone without anyone looking out for you, and you shouldn't do this alone either. Whether you can or not."

He watched her shoulders move. No doubt with those deep breaths she was forever taking. When she turned to face him, the anger in her expression was gone. But the sadness there instead wasn't any better. If anything, it was worse.

"I think the problem with us, Zeke, is we do *everything* better alone."

He wasn't sure why that should land like some kind of slap. He'd always *preferred* working alone, being alone. It was who he was. *Lone wolf*, Carlyle used to throw at him, and he'd taken that as a badge of honor.

But the way Brooke said it made it sound *sad*, and the way she stood there looking alone made him *feel* sad.

That, he wouldn't let himself marinate in. "Not this, Brooke. I'll follow you to your rental. Let's pack up your stuff. Stay with me until we get to the bottom of this. Someone is *tracking* you. You shouldn't be alone. You know that. I know you know that."

She stared at him for the longest time, like searching his face would give her the answer she needed.

But there was only one answer. Even if she didn't like it. Even if *he* didn't like it. She either had to tell the cops or she had to let him help.

"Fine," she agreed, clearly disgusted with the concession. But she'd made it. Still, she looked at him so seriously, spoke so damn seriously. "This isn't the same as last time. It can't be."

Because *last time* had gone too far. Personally. *Last time* had been a mistake. And even now, four years on, that mistake still felt raw. And a little too close to regret.

Because he remembered every second with her. The way she'd felt in his arms. The way she'd tasted. He wanted to pretend he didn't, but being with her was like wiping away all this *past*. So four years felt like nothing and the clawing, yearning need for everything she was existed right inside him.

Like it always had. Like it always would.

But it didn't matter.

Because she wasn't his. Never would be again.

So, he nodded. "I know."

Chapter Six

Brooke was glad to have the time to drive back to her rental cabin in the car by herself. It allowed her the opportunity to breathe, to center herself, and to accept she'd made the right decision.

Sure, it reminded her too much of four years ago when she'd been working on a case for North Star and had come under some threats from the murderer she'd been close to putting behind bars. When the handsome North Star operative had been assigned to her, and their whole *thing* had started.

The serious man who'd smiled like it was just for her. Who'd flirted with her before the danger. And then he'd protected her. She'd fallen in love with him. Quick and easy, so convinced it was meant to be. There'd been a bubble of time where she'd believed that was it. Love would win the day.

Ha. Ha.

She also understood now better than back then that his...protection wasn't about feelings. She'd never considered herself naïve before. She'd had a terrible, eye-opening childhood that had never once had her believing the best in anyone, let alone that *love* was some great magical thing.

But she'd thought Zeke's protection had *meant* something, because of some strange, warped naïveté inside her. Where people didn't help, didn't protect. So the fact he had meant she'd mattered to him.

Now she understood fully. Helping wasn't only intrinsic to who he was. He'd seen the entire North Star mission as one of protection. Of keeping people safe. It hadn't had to be about *her* for him to feel the need to protect. It was just all the things he was made of.

So, he *had* to protect her in this moment, regardless of any feelings he might have had or not had for her. Any old attractions that may or may not still exist between them. It didn't matter. She couldn't let it matter.

It was just…smart to let him step in and help. And protect. Because she didn't know what she was up against. And no matter how she liked to fancy herself a survivor, she'd really only *endured*, not necessarily *survived.* Never fought for herself. Or the people she should have fought for.

So she had to remember Zeke protecting her was just… a job. Even if he wouldn't let her pay him. It was a *job* he was doing. Because she needed help, and he needed to give it.

Brooke repeated that to herself a few times as she parked in front of the rental cabin she'd been so looking forward to staying at. Nestled a little out of town, bird-feeders in the yard and suncatchers in the windows. For almost a month, she'd gotten to live here and pretend it was home while she examined the skeletal remains found on the Brink farm.

If it had been only that, it would have been a nice interlude. But then the remains had been found in the cave. But then she'd felt she was being followed. But *then* she'd been the person to bring Zeke into it.

Her fault. So it was her responsibility to *endure* once again.

Zeke was out of his truck and next to her before she could even fish her keys out of her purse. He held out his hand, like he was expecting her to just hand over the keys to the cabin. Mr. In Charge. Always.

She opened her mouth to argue with him. To tell him she could take care of it. But what a waste of breath. He wanted to protect. She'd be a lot better off *letting* him, rather than fighting him on it.

Will you be better off or are you just hoping it'll be easier? Survive or endure?

She really wasn't sure about the answer. Everything was so jumbled up and hypothetical. The only thing she knew for sure was that she could not make the same mistakes she'd made four years ago.

Number one, she wouldn't read into him wanting to help. Number two, she would have boundaries. Zeke was the expert when it came to safety, so she'd allow him liberties there. But *only* when it came to safety.

So, she got her key out and ignored his outstretched hand. She walked up to the door, unlocked it herself, then gestured him inside.

He didn't frown exactly, but she could read disapproval in the lines of his face. She ignored it.

"Stay," he said sharply before taking a step inside.

It took Brooke longer than it should have to realize he was talking to the dog. She blinked at Viola then scurried inside to follow Zeke. Because she didn't need to follow anyone's orders if she didn't want to.

It didn't do thinking about if she wanted to or not.

"Anything seem out of place?" he asked, scanning the small living room and tiny kitchen that were immediately visible.

Brooke didn't look at first. There'd been a time when no

one would have had to ask her that question. When it would have been the first thing she'd do when she walked into a room. Look for what was out of place, brace herself for whatever might be wrong. Rearrange herself accordingly.

But this wasn't about her childhood in a biker cult. It wasn't even about one of those disaster foster homes. It was just straightforward danger. The kind she got for looking into dead people.

She walked through the cabin, looking for anything that struck her as wrong. Her suitcase was where she'd left it yesterday morning, organized and open. She poked her head into the bathroom. Her toiletries were lined up along the counter just as she'd left them.

"If anyone has been through my things, they were very careful."

Zeke nodded, studying the cabin. He poked at light fixtures, pushed on windows. She didn't ask what he was doing—another lesson she'd learned. She would keep herself…separate from his attempts at keeping her safe.

No teamwork. No North Star to bind them. He was *just* a bodyguard. She was determined to think of him that way. Besides, when it came to her other options—telling the detectives or staying with the Hudsons as Zeke's sister had suggested—surely figuring out how to deal with her ex-boyfriend from four years ago was better than that.

So she packed up her belongings and brought everything out to the front door. She hadn't packed heavy because she didn't have a lot of worldly possessions, even now that she was more financially stable.

Because she was too used to moving, and because her job called for so much travel, she'd convinced herself it was fine not to have a real home base. Fine to be a bit of a nomad and have a small collection of belongings that could be bundled up in less than an hour.

But it always made her far sadder than it should to see her life sorted into a single suitcase and nothing else.

In silence, Zeke hefted the bag—because why would a stubborn, ego driven man ever let her *help*—and took her things outside. Brooke followed, locking the cabin door behind her. She wouldn't get *rid* of the rental just yet. Maybe it was a waste of money, but it was always good to have a place to disappear to if needed.

She had a bad feeling she was definitely going to need that. An escape hatch, right within reach.

Zeke tossed her bag into the bed of his truck. "Let's leave your car here tonight. It might throw some people off. You've got a routine down, and we want to shake it up in the eyes of anyone who might be following."

Brooke didn't trust herself to speak and not argue, so she just nodded and headed for the truck's passenger side. She'd gotten herself into this mess. She had to take the consequences of her actions in stride. Because maybe it had been four years, but she knew Zeke too well to have thought this would go any other way.

He got in the driver's seat and she hefted herself into the passenger's, but just as she did she caught sight of something out of the corner of her eye. She looked over her shoulder. There was a gravel road out beyond the cabin. Brooke hadn't done any exploring to see where it led, but along with a minor cloud of dust, she saw a flash of silver before it disappeared into the tree line.

Her heart seemed to stop for a moment, and her legs wouldn't keep her up, so she sank into the seat, Viola hopping in behind her. "Did you see—"

"I saw it," Zeke said, his voice detached and very *mili-*

tary. A little North Star déjà vu. "Get out of the truck. Go back in the cabin and lock the door."

But that would take time, because he wouldn't leave until she was safely tucked away and the car already had too big of a head start. She pulled her truck door closed. "We both know there's no time. Just go."

He slid her one irritated glance then he hit the accelerator.

Brooke held on to Viola as they took off toward where they'd both seen the flash of a silver car.

ZEKE FOCUSED ON driving as fast as he could while also being mindful of the woman clutching the handle of the door for dear life. He didn't want to scare her, but he sure as hell didn't want to miss his chance to get to the bottom of this.

"What do we do if we catch up to him?" Brooke asked, her cool, calm voice a direct opposite to the way she clutched the door and how wide her eyes were. She always had been able to maintain that seemingly calm voice in the face of all sorts of danger.

But he was the one equipped to *deal* with all that danger. She did not have that kind of training. "You'll stay in the truck. I'll handle it."

He ignored her sigh, concentrated on taking a curve in the gravel road without flipping the truck. He saw another flash. They were gaining *some* on the car, and it helped he was in a vehicle that could handle the rough terrain and the stalker was in a sedan that was just as likely to rattle apart as it was to make it over the next gravel hill.

Zeke lost sight of the car as it crested the hill first. And he didn't like that tactical disadvantage. Still, he could hardly let the guy just disappear. Answers were within their reach, and he had to get them.

"Get my gun out of the glove compartment."

Not a sigh this time, just a noise unique to Brooke that he recognized all too well, full of disapproval. Why that made him want to smile in this tense moment was something he was going to have to excavate…some other time.

Still, she did as told, opening the glove compartment and pulling out the gun, not hiding her distaste.

"Can you hold on to it for a minute?" He had to maneuver the truck into a defensive position as he crested the hill. One that would keep Brooke out of the line of potential fire.

And quickly. The minute Zeke took his truck over the hill, the driver of the silver sedan was parked and getting out.

Zeke screeched to a stop on an angle to keep some distance, to keep Brooke not directly in the man's line of sight.

"Stay in the truck." An order for the dog…and the woman.

She didn't mount an argument, just handed over the gun.

He opened his driver's-side door, got out of the truck carefully, using the door as a kind of shield while he held his gun trained on the man—who *appeared* unarmed. Zeke suspected the driver had a firearm on him somewhere. He was way too calm with a gun pointed in his direction not to have some kind of weapon handy.

Unless he had backup. Zeke turned off the safety on his gun and scanned the world around them. He saw one rental cabin in the distance, but otherwise just highway and land. No people. No nothing.

Zeke began to move toward the driver. The guy held his hands up in surrender, though it didn't feel like a particularly scared or submissive move. It appeared far more...*mocking*.

Zeke didn't quite know what to do with this, but he'd been in strange, confusing and dangerous situations before. He'd made an entire adulthood out of it—hell, his entire life had been about getting people, including himself, out of trouble.

With his gun clearly drawn, he continued to inch toward the man. Zeke watched everything and put Brooke and the dog out of his mind. The trick to any difficult situation was to divorce feelings from it and to focus on instincts only.

He'd only ever struggled with that as a North Star agent when Brooke was involved. And she, for some reason, had reminded him of his family. Of Walker out there trying to track down their mother's killer and maybe getting himself killed in the process. Of Carlyle out there chomping at the bit. Of Walker trying to protect her from all the world had to offer.

Brooke had reminded him of what he'd felt for his family, and it had been the first chink in an armor he'd considered impenetrable. It had been the first realization he'd been getting in too deep with her.

And now was quite possibly the worst time *ever* to be thinking about that.

"It seems you've taken a real interest in my friend," Zeke called across the distance. He was close enough to take stock of the man. The guy was tall, big. Definitely wouldn't be easy to take down in a fight. They'd be almost evenly matched, and he had a fighter's kind of stance that spoke of either time in the ring or time in a cell.

Zeke was betting on the latter.

He still didn't see anyone in their surroundings. No backup. Unless he was missing something, but Zeke had to trust his instincts and believe he wasn't. While preparing for *anything*.

"You could say that," the man returned, unbothered. "And you could also say it's none of your damn business."

"You'd be wrong about that."

The guy jerked his chin toward the truck. "Then why is she getting out?"

Zeke knew better than to look, than to be distracted. He really did. He was almost certain he wouldn't have looked back, except he heard the sound of feet hitting gravel.

He wanted to shout at her, but some gut feeling he could still manage to follow caught it in time, so he said nothing at all. Though he did move his body to act as a physical barrier between Brooke's approaching form and the man.

Since she couldn't stay in the damn truck. He wanted to curse. Instead he could only watch her out of the corner of his eye. The dog followed by her side—neither bounding ahead nor lagging behind.

Brooke came to an abrupt stop a few steps behind Zeke.

"Royal?" she said. Her voice didn't seem strong enough to carry, but he noted the way the man by the car stiffened.

Zeke didn't lower the gun but glanced at Brooke, now moving toward the man, clearly without thinking. Zeke grabbed her by the arm with his free hand as she tried to pass him. She looked over at him as if startled to find him still there.

The man crossed his big, tattooed arms over his chest and *smirked* at Zeke. Then his gaze moved to Brooke.

"Heya, Chick."

Chapter Seven

For a moment, it was like being out of time. Like she wasn't a living, breathing, being anymore. Just…mist. Nothing tangible. Because this couldn't be real, so she couldn't be real.

Then Zeke had grabbed her arm, held her in place, and she'd come back together. Her mouth was dry, her hands shook, but she was breathing again. Her heart was pounding in her ears, so loud, she didn't know if Zeke was saying anything to her or not.

Because she was looking at her brother.

Brooke didn't even know why she recognized him. *How* she did. He'd been ten years old the last time she'd seen him. He'd looked so different. Small and vulnerable and decidedly untattooed, though maybe with some of the same belligerence in his expression.

Now he was…a man.

Yet there was something in the eyes. In the way he looked at her. A mix of sibling devotion and massive distrust. Even as a toddler, he'd been a dichotomy. No doubt fighting between all that evil around them and the good Brooke had tried so hard to hold on to. So hard to give him.

She'd *known* it was him in this moment, just from that look alone.

Then he'd called her "Chick," and no one else knew that nickname. Not a soul in the world. It was just theirs. And she hadn't heard it in over a decade. Hadn't *seen* him in over a decade.

Her *brother* was standing there. Right in front of her. Adult. Alive.

It was so easy to forget about everything except that. For a brief, beautiful moment she did. Forgot everything except *relief.*

They'd been separated in foster care, and Brooke had promised to find him. She'd promised. It had taken too long. Even she'd known that. Once she'd finally tracked him down—in jail for work he'd done with Sons of the Badlands, the biker cult their parents had been a part of— she'd started writing him letters. He hadn't responded, and she'd been mostly okay with that. She'd known she'd borne some responsibility for him going down that path. Hard feelings were natural.

She'd hired him a lawyer to make sure he could get out when he'd done his time. He'd never answered one of her letters. Never given her any indication he cared about her, even if he'd used the lawyer. Still, she hadn't heard he was out. She hadn't heard anything.

Now he was following her? Finding her?

There was an initial swing of elation, of love, of hope. But it was quickly soured by the reality of the situation. There was no *good* explanation for her brother to be skulking around following her. If he wanted to see her, he would have known he could contact her. He would have known she would help him with anything. Like she'd tried to do behind the scenes the past few years. He had to know that.

Didn't he?

"Aren't you going to give your baby brother a hug?" he finally said. She heard the sarcasm dripping from every word, and still she wanted to do just that. Reach out. Hold him. Assure herself he was real.

"Royal…" She started to move forward again, not necessarily to give him a hug. Not necessarily to do anything but to give him a closer look so maybe she could somehow make sense of this.

But Zeke's grip on her arm remained firm. "I don't care if you know him, Brooke," Zeke said on a whisper. "He's been stalking you."

"I can't quite figure this guy out," Royal called from where he still stood a decent distance away. "Not a husband. Not a boyfriend. Just some annoying dude skulking around. What's up with that?"

She kept forgetting Zeke was even there. She just…

She turned to Zeke, placed her free hand over the one holding her arm. "Keep your gun on him all you want, but you need to let me go."

"Brooke." The word was *pained*, not just irritated. She knew he was worried. Confused. But not any more than she was.

"Zeke. It's my brother. Royal."

"The brother you had to…" Zeke didn't say the rest. He knew the whole story of them being separated by foster care. She'd sobbed it out to him one day when they'd been together.

This, of course, did not soften Zeke any to Royal. Because Zeke knew he'd been involved in the Sons and ended up in jail, though she'd never gotten into the nitty-gritty of why. She'd known Zeke would never believe her brother's innocence. No, innocence and being involved in a gang wouldn't make sense to a man like Zeke.

But by some miracle she'd have to think about later, Zeke actually released her arm. He did not drop the gun from pointing at her brother, but he let her go.

She'd owe him for that alone.

Brooke didn't run to her brother. She knew better than to think this could all be solved by a hug even if her hands itched to grab onto him. To hold on. To assure herself he was alive and well.

But he wasn't a little boy anymore, and she'd failed him. Still, she moved closer. Studying every change. The square jaw, the crooked nose, the tattoos, the scars. So few glimpses of a little boy she'd tried to raise with some semblance of right and wrong. Some inkling of love.

"Royal. What are you *doing* here? How…? Why…?"

He looked at her a long time, his gaze cold. "You told me you'd come get me, Chick. You never did."

"I tried," she said, her voice more rusty than she wanted.

He snorted. Like he didn't believe her. Like she hadn't sent those letters, that lawyer. Like…

"You were in jail, honey. Didn't you get my letters?" She didn't understand how he wouldn't have known it was her. Even though she hadn't been allowed to have contact with him—first because of his sentencing, then because of her involvement with North Star—the letters were supposed to get through. "Who do you think hired that lawyer?"

A small line appeared in his forehead, but his expression was one of distrust. That was…hurtful, when she probably didn't have any right to be hurt.

"That guy…"

Brooke didn't look back at Zeke, though tempted. "Is a friend. And someone who wants to help me. Help me not get *stalked*, Royal."

"I wasn't stalking. I was…" He took a step closer, reached out, but Viola, at Brooke's side, began to growl low in her throat. Royal stopped in his tracks and flicked a glance down at the dog. "Guard dog, huh?"

"Royal." She couldn't be distracted. She had to know. "Why have you been following me?"

Royal glanced at Zeke, still holding that ridiculous gun pointed at her brother. Royal leaned in close, eyes on the dog, waiting for her to growl again.

"Something isn't right," he said, quiet enough Zeke wouldn't be able to hear. "I don't know what it is, but I have a bad feeling it's got to do with Dad." His expression was hard, detached, but she didn't think he was lying. And the mention of their father had a cold ball of dread settling in her gut. "And I was worried enough it had to do with you to come looking."

"You could have told me. You could have…" But no use going down the road of all the things he could have done. She could have done. Sometimes you could only deal with what *was*, not what could have been.

With Zeke and Royal suddenly back in her life, she was really going to have to learn that lesson.

He shook his head. "Best if you don't get mixed up with me, Chick. Unless it's too late." He sighed. "I'm starting to think it's too late."

THE ONLY THING that kept Zeke from rushing closer, from grabbing Brooke and getting her the hell out of there, was the memory of the way she'd cried over the brother she'd thought she'd failed.

He knew too much about the complicated feelings sibling relationships brought out. The way love didn't dim over mistakes and disagreements. Maybe even when it should.

So Zeke watched, his finger still on the trigger of the gun, ready for anything. He wasn't about to trust the guy just because Brooke shared genetics with him.

Brooke and Royal exchanged a few quiet words Zeke couldn't make out, and then she turned and walked toward him. Zeke searched Brooke's face for a second or two before he reminded himself it was her brother he needed to be paying attention to. That her brother might be a threat.

He wouldn't say she looked happy, but she seemed *awed* to see her brother there. Definitely surprised.

Royal stood by his silver sedan, arms still crossed over his chest, belligerent look still on his face. But he watched Brooke go. There was definitely no awe on his face, but *something* had Zeke carefully lowering his gun.

One of the things all the veterans of North Star had impressed upon him when he'd been young and eager, and they'd had years of missions under their belts, was to trust *all* your instincts. Not just the cynical ones. The ones that wanted to see the bad, the evil in everyone just because some existed in the world.

If you didn't allow for the good and hopeful instincts, you weren't that far removed from the bad you were trying to stop in the world.

When Brooke approached, she tried to smile at him, but it faltered. "He, um, didn't want to see me, but he wanted to make sure I was okay."

Zeke knew he should keep his feelings on that to himself, but… "That doesn't make any sense."

She shook her head. "No. Maybe not. But I gave him the keys to my rental. He can stay there tonight, and I'll stay with you and then maybe I'll… Well, I'll have time to think this over, decide how to move forward. But I'm not being stalked, so there is that."

"You *are* being stalked, Brooke. Just because it's your brother doesn't mean it's not…" His words fell off because she'd closed her eyes as if in pain.

Because no doubt she didn't need *him* to tell her that her brother might be dangerous. So, best to just…get her out of here. Maybe back at the ranch they could really take stock of the situation, and if they knew where Royal was and he wasn't following Brooke, all the better.

"Okay. Let's head home, huh?"

She hesitated a moment and then nodded. He helped her into the truck and she let him, which was a worry in itself. But Viola wiggled her way into the truck, laying her big head on Brooke's shoulder.

Neither Brooke nor Zeke said a word to one another as he drove them back to his ranch. It was dark now. A bright quarter moon hung in the sky over his house when he pulled up. He thrust the gear into Park, shut off the engine, and got out.

Viola jumped out after him, but Brooke didn't immediately follow. Zeke didn't move forward onto the porch and instead waited for Brooke while Viola ran off into the dark.

Eventually Brooke opened the door and carefully climbed out of the truck, moving like she was injured and afraid to jostle whatever was hurting.

He had to fight the urge to move back to the truck and help her down. Touch her in some reassuring way. She'd had a shock, was still confused, and no doubt hurting, but that had nothing to do with him.

She needed to deal with this on her own.

So, he walked up onto the porch. Viola bounded up

from whatever she'd been off doing. Stiffly, Brooke followed. She didn't even lean down to pet Viola when the dog pressed against her.

He unlocked the door, trying not to stare at her to try to read every little emotion in her eyes. "I've got a frozen pizza I can heat up for us." He pushed the door open and ushered her inside.

She moved in, still acting like a stray breeze might blow her to pieces. "I think I'll just go to sleep."

"Brooke, you haven't had any dinner. You have to eat something."

"I'm not..." Her breathing hitched. "Hungry," she said on a voice that cracked. She shook her head, as if she could shake her tears away, but they began to fall.

He couldn't take it. So many things he could withstand. Pain. Torture. Manipulation. Aggression. You name it.

But her tears undid him.

"Sweetheart." He moved for her, pulled her into his arms. And much like she had all those years ago when she'd told him about her brother, she sobbed into his shoulder.

"He didn't even know I tried. That I was the one who hired the lawyer. Why wouldn't he know that?"

"I don't know," Zeke replied, rubbing her back, holding her close. Trying and failing to put all those old feelings on ice. Because she leaned into him, just like she used to. Like she trusted him. Like she believed he could be the protector she deserved.

It cracked too many things inside him, and even knowing he should push the feelings aside, set her aside, he couldn't. He brushed some hair out of her face because it was sticking to the tears.

She looked up at him. Their gazes held. Hers wet and

blue. Too soft, too trusting. Too…much everything. And they just stood in that moment. His heart beating hard, her cheeks turning an alluring shade of pink.

And now was not the time for any of *that*, so he forced himself to speak.

"We'll figure it out though." The words came out rough.

She let out a shaky breath then swallowed and squeezed her eyes shut. She shook her head. "No, I don't think we should." She wriggled away from him.

"Brooke."

She wiped her face, stepped back, and fixed him with a pathetic attempt at a smile. A smile meant to keep him at arm's length. A smile meant to prove nothing was still there.

When there *was*. But this new development had also thrown her for a loop.

"I can't… He's my brother. I messed up. But I also know some part of him blames me for things. I don't think I should go poking around. I think I should let him…have the time and space to decide if he wants to tell me."

Maybe she was right. In a lot of other situations, he'd agree with her. But… "Brooke, he was following you. I don't care what he said, it wasn't just to make sure you're okay. He could have seen that the first day he followed you. It's been what? Three days?"

She hesitated. Only for a second or two, but he saw it all the same. "Well, sure, but—"

"Jesus, Brooke. How long had it been going on before you came to me?"

She shrugged jerkily. "I wasn't sure at first."

At first. So God knew how long her brother had been watching. God knew how long this had been going on and she'd just…let it. "Did being part of North Star teach you anything?"

Her gaze cooled. Even with those tears still on her cheeks, her expression went full ice. "Oh, it taught me plenty."

He reached out for her. "Sweetheart—"

"Stop that," she snapped, sidestepping his arm. "*Sweetheart*. I don't want you to call me that ever again."

That was fair but landed like a blow all the same. "Sorry." Hell, he was botching this six ways to Sunday. Because that's what happened when you did something stupid like *care* about the people involved in dangerous situations. Messed up. Ruined things. Hurt people you didn't mean to hurt.

And still, he didn't know how to keep his distance, because *someone* had to look out for her. When it came to her brother, she had too soft a heart and it was going to get her a lot more hurt than whatever mistakes he might make when it came to her.

She already wasn't taking care of herself, which he tried to use as fodder to piss him off enough to put those walls back up. "You're going to eat something. You don't have to share a table with me, but you're going to eat."

"I'm not your responsibility, Zeke. I know that's what your North Star training told you, but it's wrong. I don't *need* you to worry about me, take care of me, save me."

As if he'd do it if *he* didn't *need* to. As if he'd be standing here with his heart raw and obnoxious if he didn't *need* her to be okay. As if he hadn't spent the past four years keeping tabs on her for that very reason.

That, she didn't know, and it wouldn't do to tell her. "I wish I could feel that way, Brooke."

She closed her eyes and sighed. "I don't want to fight with you. I just…"

"You're going to sit down and eat, and then you're going to get some sleep. We can talk through next steps in the morning." Because she needed those things.

And he needed some space to get a hold of himself so he could be what she needed. So she would be safe, and when everything was all said and done, go back to whatever life she had out there that didn't involve him.

And rightfully so.

Chapter Eight

In the morning, Brooke left.

Not for good. Just early enough that *hopefully* Zeke wouldn't know what she'd done. Of course, she'd had to take his truck, so it was unlikely she wasn't going to have to explain herself, but she had to do this first.

At the sheriff's department. Maybe Zeke would know she'd done *something*, but she didn't have to tell him exactly what. It was none of his business. Royal was none of his business. No matter how kind he'd been about the whole thing yesterday.

Brooke had never had a *normal* life. Nothing had ever really been easy or routine or settled. The only routine was that unexpected change would inevitably come knocking.

Zeke.

Her brother.

Her *father*.

She still couldn't quite believe what Royal had told her. She should have told Zeke. The guilt was eating her up. Staying in his house, eating his food, and keeping this huge secret.

Yet she would also feel guilty if she told Zeke something Royal didn't want shared.

And at the end of the day, she wasn't sure who the right

man to place her loyalty with was. They'd both hurt her in different ways. She'd failed them both in different ways.

Maybe you should just bail.

Tempting. So tempting. Retreat. Isolate. She wanted to. It was the right thing. Everyone was getting too deep and too complicated and too hard.

But she had a job to do. So she didn't choose Zeke or Royal. She'd decided to choose someone who had no *real* connection to her. It was hard to ask for help. It made her feel sick to her stomach. A burden and a bother, when she wanted to handle everything herself.

Nonetheless, she couldn't handle this. So she walked into the sheriff's department and asked for Thomas. She was pretty sure he had an early morning shift to cover her morning cave work, and when the administrative assistant took her through the security measures and then directed her to his office, she let out a slow, steady breath.

This was going to work. This was going to be okay. The police were there to help, and Thomas had been nothing but kind. Besides, she wasn't asking for anything difficult.

His office door was open and he sat at his desk, writing something down on a piece of paper.

"Thomas."

He looked up from his desk, no doubt surprised to see her. He glanced at the clock. "Did I miss a schedule change?" he asked with some concern.

She managed a smile and shook her head. "No. I have a favor to ask you. As a detective. Not related to the cave or the remains."

The concern didn't leave his expression. He pointed to the seat in his office. "Sit."

Brooke didn't let her nerves show. There was nothing

to be nervous about. She was only asking for a favor. *Information*. And once she had it, she could decide what to do about Royal's theories. What to do about Zeke.

Thomas was not the kind of guy to hold it against her, and if it hurt Zeke's feelings that she was asking someone else for help, that was his problem. And if Royal was going to get bent out of shape over her finding the truth... Well.

The only thing that mattered was the truth. The facts. The data from which she could then make an educated choice.

"I don't know what kind of background you guys did into me when I was hired for this case," she began, because she'd been internally practicing this interaction ever since the idea had occurred to her last night.

"Not much. We needed a forensic anthropologist ASAP. I think maybe someone looked into your credentials, but that was all bureaucratic red tape I'm not involved in. So I can't say as I know much."

No doubt because there wasn't much to know. No doubt Zeke had gone through Granger to refer her to Bent County when his friends had needed a forensic anthropologist, which meant Granger had used his *skills* to smooth over anything standing in her way of helping.

Not that she wasn't qualified for the job, or her cases wouldn't speak for themselves. Just that the governmental wheels in place for these things tended to run a little slow, and this had been quick. North Star—or Granger MacMillan—interference quick.

And now *she* had to be quick and get to the point. "My father was a high-ranking member of the Sons of the Badlands." She couldn't believe she was still talking about this all these years later. Almost five years since the Sons had been wiped out.

"That old biker gang?" Thomas responded, eyebrows drawn together as if he couldn't remember. Or couldn't believe it.

She nodded. "Yes. I was under the impression he was in jail. For life. But... I heard a rumor. I just want to know where he's at. What the state of his sentencing is. I thought maybe you would be able to get that information or know someone who would."

Thomas nodded. "Absolutely. Are you worried about your safety?"

She shook her head. "No, nothing like that. Not really. I never really mattered to him. But my brother... I do worry about him. It would just ease my mind to know everything is as it should be."

"Okay. I just need his name and a few other details and I should be able to have some answers to you by the end of the day." He picked up a pen and pulled a pad of paper in front of him. He asked for the normal things. Name. Birth date. What jail she thought he was in.

Brooke recited the information as best she could even though speaking her father's name made her feel...fragile.

Once Thomas was done, he tapped his pen to the pad, studying the information. He was quiet for a long moment before looking up, meeting her gaze. "Did you talk to Zeke about this?"

That surprised her enough to frown at him. "This is none of Zeke's business." She tried not to sound irritated.

"Isn't that his truck you drove up here?"

She wasn't sure how Thomas knew what she'd driven to the station, but she didn't like it. She stood, probably too abruptly. "I don't need you to poke into it. I just need to know the facts. I thought I could trust you to get them and relay them."

He never looked away from her, never let her agitation get to him. He was all cop-calm as he held her angry gaze. "You can," he said seriously.

She almost sagged with relief. It didn't take the stress away but did loosen some of the tight band it had created around her shoulders.

But then, Thomas kept talking about *Zeke*.

"You and I might not be friends, Brooke, but I *am* friends with Zeke. I don't think there's anything worth keeping from him if it's dangerous. For what it's worth, he's a good guy and he can keep you safe, if you're in danger."

"I'm not in danger," she said firmly. Because she *wasn't*. Royal was just… She didn't know, but she wasn't involved with Royal's recent past. "It's ancient history."

"You of all people should know just how dangerous ancient history is."

That felt far too ominous for comfort.

She turned to leave. Because she'd done what she'd come to do, and he was going to help her. She'd asked for help and gotten it, and the world hadn't ended. So there. "I'll see you at the cave later."

Because the job went on. No matter what Royal thought was going on with their father.

ZEKE HAD WOKEN to an empty house and his truck missing. He wasn't sure what took precedence. His anger she'd gone off and done something stupid and dangerous, no matter what it was. Or the fact he hadn't woken up.

What kind of operative was he?

The retired kind?

He pushed that thought out of his head. He assumed Brooke's secret trip was to see her brother, so he'd called

Walker and asked to borrow one of his cars. Carlyle had driven the old junker over, and he owed her one.

That was annoying.

Zeke drove to Brooke's rental cabin, concerned the car might not make it. Walker had to be keeping this clunker for sentimental reasons instead of practical ones. There was no way he'd let Mary drive this thing with the baby. And at the rate they were going, they'd need a minivan soon.

By the time he made it to Brooke's rental, she was already gone. Or, *maybe*, he'd been wrong about where she'd gone. He didn't think so. He knew her. He understood her.

And now it was his turn to have a little conversation with her brother. One *she* didn't get to hear.

Before Zeke had turned off the engine, Royal stood at the door. His arms were crossed over his chest again, but he didn't have a weapon. Zeke considered holstering his, but instead, as a sign of good faith, he left it in the car.

Or maybe, in the back of his mind, he worried what Brooke would think about him showing up armed if it got back to her. Not that he intended to tell her about this, but Royal might.

And that was fine. It was all *fine*. He was just making it clear to this man that whatever he was up to wasn't something Zeke would allow Brooke to be caught in the middle of.

He got out of the car and made his way up to the door of the cabin. He'd left Viola back at the ranch with Carlyle in case Brooke returned in his absence.

"Didn't realize my morning would start with a visit from Brooke's bodyguard."

"You know, speaking as a brother, I'd be pretty happy

if someone was looking out for my sister at any point, but especially when someone was sneaking around following her."

"Looking out for her, huh?" Royal replied. "I'm not the only one who's been following her. I saw you at the cave."

That's different, he wanted to say, but knew it would be hard to explain *how* it was different. Because he hadn't told her that was what he'd been doing when he'd followed her around. "Your sister came to me for help. I plan to give it."

"What exactly did Brooke tell you?" Royal asked suspiciously.

"That you told her you've been following her because you wanted to make sure she was okay, which is BS, obviously. Stalking isn't concern."

"That all she tell you?"

Zeke didn't like the idea of there being more, but he had to play it casual. "What else is there?"

Royal shook his head. "Nothing. Look, I don't have anything to do with you and you don't have anything to do with me. Whatever you're trying to do—intimidate me?—it's not going to work. So why don't you just leave me alone?"

"Here's the bottom line. I'm not letting anything happen to her. Whether that's protecting her from you or whatever else, it's not happening. It's best if you know that, straight off."

"What? So I can run away like I'm scared of some…" He looked Zeke up and down. "Rancher?"

Zeke smiled at him. "You should be."

Royal's gaze was more considering than it had been. "You military or something?" he asked.

"Was for a time. Among other things."

Royal nodded as if satisfied with that answer. "That's good, I guess. I happen to think prison offers a better training ground for understanding a criminal enough to stop him, but knowing how to use a gun has its plusses."

"That it does."

Silence settled between them. No doubt Royal was taking Zeke's measure, the same way Zeke was doing to him. But Zeke knew Royal had no concept of who he was. Zeke had heard stories of Royal as a kid, and the ways Brooke felt she'd failed him after they'd been separated in foster care.

He also knew that a childhood like theirs made trouble more common than not. He'd been on the edge of it himself a time or two, but Walker had always pulled him back from the edge. Instilled in him the importance of doing the right thing...for the family.

Where would he have been if they'd all been separated?

He didn't appreciate the wriggle of compassion he felt for Royal. There was no reason to trust him, but that didn't mean he couldn't have a certain level of empathy toward him. It didn't mean he couldn't make the first move. "I've known Brooke a long time," he said, hoping to give some context to why he was here, and what he'd do to keep Brooke safe from anyone.

Even her brother.

Royal shrugged. "I knew her first."

"You knew a girl. I know the woman she is. And I know how it killed her to find out you were in jail, that you never responded to all those letters, and I know she blamed herself for all of it."

"You sure know a lot."

"Damn straight."

"But you know her side. Maybe from my side she *should* blame herself."

Zeke didn't let his hands curl into fists, though they wanted to. "And maybe she shouldn't. You were both dealt the same shitty hand, and I hate to break it to you, lots of people are. She figured out how to build a real life out of it. You can blame her for that, or you can build your own. But nothing's going to happen to her. I won't let it. So I don't know why you're here, why you've been following her, but it's not going to get past me. You can believe me, or you can run up against me, but Brooke won't be the target."

There was a long, drawn-out pause while Royal studied him and Zeke stood there, letting him.

"You care about her," Royal said after a while, like he wasn't completely sure he believed it. Like it was a question.

"You're damn right." Because what was the point hemming and hawing to her brother? What was the point ignoring it himself? Maybe he hated it. Maybe he wished he didn't. But he did and it wasn't going away. *So.*

"Good. Someone should."

Zeke could only stare at the one person he'd ever seen Brooke cry over, besides his own sorry ass. Multiple times. "Her brother could."

"I could," he agreed. His expression remained grim but wasn't quite so abrasive. "If I thought it was safe. But it's not. And neither is she."

That sounded somehow both like a warning and a threat.

"How so?"

"If she wanted you to know, you'd know."

That was fair, even if it hurt.

"Does *she* know?"

Royal smirked. "You care about her but she's not telling you her secrets?" He tsked. "Maybe you're not quite as important to her as you'd like to think."

"I shouldn't be important to her at all." He shouldn't have said that out loud. Besides, he'd come here to warn Royal, and now he had. What the guy did with said warning was up to him.

Zeke turned to leave, trying not to concern himself with Brooke's *secrets*. Because she could tell him or not tell him whatever she wanted. It was her life. Her family.

Her safety—that is your responsibility.

"Hey."

Zeke stopped, turned to face Royal, who still stood on the porch.

"Look up what I was in jail for." Then he turned on a heel and disappeared inside, the slam of the cabin door echoing through the quiet morning.

Zeke wasn't sure what kind of parting shot that was, but it was…interesting.

And, surely, Hart could get him Royal's entire rap sheet. So, he hopped in his borrowed car and decided to head for Bent. Maybe he could catch the detective before he headed out to the caves to meet up with Brooke.

He started driving, his thoughts fixing on Royal Campbell and jail, on the fact the brother Brooke hadn't seen in something like fifteen years might know something about her Zeke didn't.

He kept picturing yesterday. When Brooke and Royal had spoken quietly and Zeke hadn't heard what they'd said. He'd chalked it up to sibling stuff.

But what if it was more and she was hiding something big from him?

Before he could give that too much thought, he saw a truck going in the opposite direction on its side of the highway, which was normal.

Except that it was *his* truck.

Chapter Nine

Brooke couldn't imagine getting back to Zeke's ranch before he woke up. She'd have to explain taking his truck, where she'd gone, what she'd been doing.

Or you could tell him to butt out.

She snorted. Yeah, that'd work. Well, she'd just have to lie. As much as she didn't like the idea, telling him she'd been out doing errands wasn't a *full* lie.

She just had to know the facts before she could proceed. And he'd want to proceed with *no* facts. She needed data. He just went on instinct. This was too…big for that. Too personal. Too hers.

This whole morning had been nothing but instinct, and it was already a disaster.

When she turned into the drive of Zeke's ranch, she slowed his truck along the drive because someone was in front of the house. Someone was outside, playing fetch with the dog.

At first, Brooke could make out the shape of what was a woman with dark hair. Something a little too close to hot twisting jealousy poked her right in the chest. That was *ridiculous*. Zeke had made it clear he hadn't been seeing anyone.

Not that it mattered.

Something she could fully assure herself of when she finally got close enough to recognize the woman as Zeke's sister. Maybe she was there to take Viola back? Brooke hadn't left the dog outside this morning. That meant Zeke was awake, but still inside, and…

Now she'd have to explain her disappearance to both of them. *That* was what she got for going on instinct and running out of the house this morning. If she'd really thought it through, planned it out, been *careful,* she wouldn't be in this mess.

Data, examination and the careful drawing of conclusions was always the answer. Go figure, proximity to Zeke once again left her making all the wrong choices.

She parked the truck and got out, forcing herself to smile at Carlyle. "Good morning."

"Hey. I was just in the neighborhood and thought I'd check in on Viola." She gestured at the prancing dog. Brooke frowned though. There was no car, no truck. How had Carlyle gotten here?

"How's she working out for you?" Carlyle asked as Viola eagerly put her head under Brooke's hand in greeting.

"She's great," Brooke replied with feeling. She gave Viola a pat. She did really enjoy having the dog around, not that she could let herself get used to it.

"Good." Carlyle nodded and an awkward silence followed while Carlyle fidgeted. Stepping from side to side, rocking back on her heels, decidedly not leaving or saying anything else.

Until she finally blurted, "I don't know why my brother would call me out here, because he knows I can't keep my mouth shut. What's the deal with you two?"

Brooke blinked. "Deal?"

"Yeah, like it's all tense and weird between you two, or was before. Is it because you two knew each other before? When he was doing his secret spy stuff. That's how he got a forensic whatever you are to come out here so quick when they found…" She paused and wrinkled her nose. "I never know what to call it, considering it was my fiancé's parents."

Right, because the connections here in Sunrise and Bent County were complex and complicated. Luckily, Brooke didn't have to respond to whatever Carlyle was trying to get at because a very old not-in-good-shape car roared up the drive.

Brooke startled, but she noticed Carlyle didn't so much as blink. Brooke might have grabbed for Carlyle, suggested they run, because clearly this was danger come calling, except she quickly realized Zeke was the driver.

Uh-oh.

The car squealed to a stop a little ways behind his truck, and he was out almost before the entire vehicle had stopped. He marched over to them, pointing at Carlyle, and, for a second, Brooke figured that was who he was mad at.

"Leave," he said between clenched teeth to his sister, handing her off the keys he'd had in his hand.

Okay, so maybe he wasn't mad at Carlyle. She didn't know why he was *mad* like this at *her*. She wasn't sure she'd ever seen him *mad* like this. Usually he was a controlled kind of mad. Icy.

This was…not ice.

Carlyle held up her hands in mock surrender and maybe she was trying not to grin, but Brooke didn't think she was trying *that* hard.

"And miss the show?" she asked Zeke.

He made a noise, close to a growl, which had Carlyle laughing and snatching the keys from him before moving for the old car. She paused next to Brooke though. "Oh, Brooke, he's got it *bad*. I hope you twist the knife."

Brooke wasn't sure she understood Carlyle's meaning, but then again, she wasn't sure Carlyle understood what was really going on here.

And it didn't matter, because now she had to deal with angry Zeke, which didn't seem fair. "I cannot fathom why you're this angry," Brooke said, trying to sound bored and calm. "I just borrowed your truck for a quick errand."

"An errand or a secret?" he demanded.

She wasn't sure how he could see through her so easily, and she might have felt guilty, except *he'd* been somewhere.

"Where were *you*?"

"Well, once I realized my truck was gone, I borrowed one of my brother's cars and drove to your rental, because I figured you were headed out to deal with your brother very purposefully without me."

It hadn't even occurred to her to go talk to Royal until she had more information. Until she had the *facts*.

"You didn't go there at all, did you?" He seemed so hurt by that, when it wasn't like she'd lied to him and told him she had or was going to. That was just some assumption he'd made.

"No," she replied. "I just had an errand to run." She wasn't going to explain herself. She didn't have to. She wasn't in danger anymore. Not from the thing he thought she was anyway. And before she introduced any new possibilities, she had to know…

She had to *know*. So she could protect herself first and, if after that, she needed his help, maybe she'd ask for it.

But she'd have the data first, damn it. No more instincts for her. Those had only led her astray.

And she could ask for his help, she could accept his help, but she could not *depend* on him again. On *any-one* again. Things went best when she only depended on herself.

The man in front of her, case in point. Standing there looking like…like she'd never *seen* him. Because this was a bit like a man…holding on by a thread. When he had always, *always*, been in complete and utter control.

She didn't like it, but it did make her feel sorry for him. It made her want to *soothe*.

"Zeke." She moved forward, not quite sure what she was going to do, just following that need inside her. One she'd just seconds ago been telling herself she wouldn't listen to.

But Zeke shook his head, a nonverbal *stay back*. Because he was getting himself under control or trying to.

"What was your brother in jail for?" he asked quietly and calmly.

The question made little sense in the grand scheme of things. What was he getting at? What could that have to do with anything?

Since she couldn't fathom where he was going with this, she hedged. Because she knew if she tried to defend Royal, it would only make him look more guilty. "A few different charges."

"List them, Brooke."

She didn't have to. She *didn't*. But she just…couldn't stop herself. "Do you remember the child trafficking case in the Sons that North Star was part of stopping? You would have been too new to be on the team that dealt with it, but I think you were with North Star by then."

"South Dakota, right? Shay and Cody Wyatt leading the charge?"

She nodded. She didn't know much about it herself. She just remembered Betty Wagner, North Star's resident doctor and one of Brooke's close friends at North Star, being pretty shaken up by the findings.

"What does that have to do with your brother's jail time, Brooke?"

"Royal was arrested just a little before that. On a murder charge. There was a fight with another Sons's member, and the other man died. The other man who'd been hurting those girls. But the Sons knew how to pick and choose who it got out of legal trouble. How to make sure the ones they saw as traitors saw the inside of a cell."

"You're saying a member of the Sons of the Badlands was arrested and it wasn't fair? The gang member was innocent?"

She hated how ridiculous he made it sound, because her brother *had* been a member of the Sons at that point. She knew how naïve it sounded to believe he was in there to try and stop some of the things they'd seen growing up, yet she couldn't help but hope her brother's motivations had been at least partly honorable.

And if she was wrong…well, so be it.

This was why she hadn't wanted to tell Zeke about it. Because she knew how it sounded. She also knew her brother, or tried to tell herself she did. He could find his own trouble, certainly, but he wasn't a murderer.

She wouldn't let herself believe he was a murderer as long as there was no concrete proof. She knew the case, thanks to her North Star connections at the time. It had been stacked against Royal from the start, with the help of too many people who'd ended up having Sons ties.

"Why do you think Granger agreed to help me with the funds to hire a lawyer?" she asked Zeke instead. Because everyone respected Granger, but some of the younger guys had looked up to him like a father figure.

Just like she had.

"He has a soft spot for you."

Brooke rolled her eyes. Granger had a soft spot for *any* of the people who came into North Star because they had been some kind of victim of the Sons of the Badlands. But he was also a stickler for right and wrong. "Because he knew as well as I did that Royal was in jail for trying to stop something. And I know you won't believe that—"

"Did Granger believe it?"

"Yes. After he looked through the case, he came to believe it." Maybe she'd always wondered if he'd said that just to make her feel better, but she wasn't about to admit that to Zeke.

"Then I believe it."

She let out a long breath, not quite sure how that just took all the wind out of her sails. Never in a million years had she expected it to be that easy, but she should have known. For all of them, Granger MacMillan had been and maybe even still was a kind of hero figure. No one wanted to think about him being wrong.

"I don't know how Royal feels about the charge, the trial, his jail time. I don't know what he'd say if I asked about it. I only know that all the evidence pointed to Royal protecting one of those girls. But the Sons was stronger back then, had more hands in legal pockets. And the legal system was eager to have any of them behind bars—rightfully so. I've always just been grateful the Sons got him arrested rather than kill him."

Brooke shuddered to think about how easily that psychotic cult leader could have just ended Royal's life and that's all she would have ever known. A life cut short.

She'd never know if Royal alive was their father's sad attempt to protect him, or if there was more to it. It didn't matter.

Royal was alive, and now he was here. Talking about the danger she might be in from their father. Talking to Zeke apparently. "Why did you ask me that?"

"He told me to look up why he was in jail."

Brooke didn't understand why her brother would do that, but that was nothing new. The men in her life continued to be obnoxious, ridiculous mysteries.

"Brooke, how am I going to protect you if you run off and never tell me the truth?" he asked, sounding *pained*. Hurt. Not mad at all. Just exasperated, like she was making things hard on him.

That made her feel small, and a bit like running away for good. "I'm not your burden, Zeke." She wouldn't be anyone's burden ever again. "If Royal has been the one following me, I don't need protecting the way I thought I did."

ZEKE WAS GOING about this all wrong. He knew that. He knew how touchy she was about *burdens*, even if she didn't. "You'll never be a burden to me, Brooke." And it was scary just how true that was. "Wanting to protect you is no burden."

"You don't need to," she said, refusing to believe him. Clearly. "Royal is not a threat to me, and it appears there are no other threats at the moment," she returned. As if choosing each word carefully. As if placating a small child who didn't understand complex thoughts.

Zeke didn't groan out loud, though he considered it.

But he'd gotten his blazing anger under control. Or close, anyway.

Royal had been the one to say she wasn't safe this morning. Maybe she believed she was safe now, and maybe he should let her believe that, but…something didn't add up. Because she had been *somewhere*.

"Where did you go this morning, Brooke?"

She didn't look away from him. She didn't try to lie— he would have seen through that easily enough. She just shook her head. "It's none of your business."

He nodded, that tenuous grasp on control barely holding on by a thread. She was right. It was none of his business. She didn't want him to keep her safe. She didn't want to be *safe*. Fine.

"It's not some personal insult, Zeke. It's just not about you." She didn't say that with any bite. No imperious looks. She was trying to be reasonable.

"Must be nice," he muttered, because he didn't know how to divorce *her* from anything he was feeling, doing. He didn't know how to look at her and say anything was *not about her*.

She reached out, touched his arm. "Zeke."

He knew she was going to try to soothe or comfort him. And, no. He wasn't letting her do that thing she did. Where she smoothed everything over because she hated people to be upset. Where she tried to make everything okay because she'd been failed by so many adults growing up she thought it was her sworn duty to make sure everyone around her was *okay*. Down to the bones she excavated everywhere she went.

But when she looked up at him with those sympathetic blue eyes, when she touched his arm like she could brush away this conflicting, painful fight inside him, he found he didn't want to be happy. He didn't want to be soothed, and he didn't want her to feel like that was her responsibility.

But he did want something.

Her. And he kept stepping away from that. For her own good and for his. But maybe… There was no good. Only messy pain she couldn't fix with a soothing touch or his name said in soft, compassionate tones.

Maybe there was only breaking down that wall. That's how he'd dealt with this *conflict* inside him last time. Burned it all down. So…

"To hell with it," he muttered. None of his business. Wrong person, wrong time, wrong *everything*, and still he'd spent the past four years haunted by the memory of a woman *he'd* set aside.

Because of *this*. The way she broke down his walls, defenses. Crumbled his control without even trying. He curled his hand around her head and pulled her in, crashing his mouth to hers.

She didn't even have the good sense to stiffen or to push him away. She *melted* to him on some sigh that seemed to say *finally*. Or maybe that was just him.

Finally. Finally. Finally. Four years had been too long without the taste of her, the feel of her, just *her*. And wasn't that what made everything these past few days so difficult? He knew she was in trouble, but all he wanted was *her*.

The kiss was everything it had always been. That wild heat. That sweet comfort. Mixed up in one perfect package that had never made any sense to him. Because she felt like coming home, when he'd never had one of those in the first place. Never wanted one.

She wrapped her arms around his neck and it could

have easily been four years ago. When they were together. When he'd been stupid enough to think he could control what was happening. When the idea of a *girlfriend* had been kind of novel, with the potential to be exactly what he wanted.

And nothing he didn't.

Remembering that lack of control she brought out in him had him easing back. He hadn't meant to kiss her. He hadn't meant to get angry. He hadn't *meant* any of this, and she was the only person in his whole life who'd ever mixed him up this way.

She blinked at him, arms still looped around his neck, eyes cloudy with desire and confusion and *hell*. There'd been no point to this, he supposed, but wasn't about to say that.

"It's the same," he said, his voice rough but certain. Because he wouldn't let her deny that like she did with the truth. No talk of burdens, because this had never been a burden.

It had been a wrecking ball.

"It's damn well the same, and I'm tired of pretending like it's not."

With that, he turned and stalked away. Because he couldn't just stand there and keep pretending, and that's what she wanted. To pretend everything was fine, to pretend that kiss didn't mean anything—that *he* didn't mean anything.

And, hell, he was used to that, wasn't he?

Chapter Ten

Brooke stood in the front yard of Zeke's house with Viola prancing around her for a long while, not sure what had just happened. Today. The past few days. Maybe her entire adult life.

Her body was still a riot of heat and want, and her mind whirled with confusion.

The same. Oh, boy, was it. Their chemistry hadn't waned or changed. She wasn't sure she'd really thought it *had*, but the angry way he'd thrown it out there suggested that *he* had. And he wasn't too happy about it.

She almost laughed. Maybe it was wrong, but having a better handle on their situation than he did was somewhat comforting. *She* certainly hadn't initiated any physical contact. *He'd* been the one to comfort her when she'd cried over Royal. *He'd* been the one to grab her and kiss her.

Brooke blew out a long breath. She couldn't ruminate on a kiss when she had work to get to. When she had responsibilities, and her brother, and the threat he thought their father posed. She could not put those aside because she was still hung up on her ex, who just happened to be protecting her because of some strange turn of events.

So, she needed to get ready for work. But before she could, a Bent County Sheriff's Department cruiser bumped down the gravel drive. She saw Thomas behind the wheel, so she walked over to greet him.

He didn't get out of the car but rolled down his window. "I'm headed out to the Hudson Ranch to talk to Chloe Brink about the scrapbook you found, and I was wondering if you'd come with me. It'll put us a little behind schedule on your excavation, but I think you could help here."

"Oh." The Hudson Ranch. She'd been there once. When Detective Delaney-Carson had informed the Hudson family that they'd positively identified last month's discovered remains as the long-missing parents of the Hudson clan. Brooke had gone along at the detective's request. Since the family was full of police officers and investigators, Laurel had assumed they'd have a lot of questions about the procedures that only the forensic anthropologist on the case could answer.

It had been…awful. Oh, the Hudsons had all handled the news calmly. They'd known it was coming. Still, watching so many people have to sort through their grief, no matter how anticipated, had been…painful. Usually, she was in the background of that part of what she did, not the front lines.

"There were some pictures in the scrapbook that I think are *in* the cave, or near it," Thomas explained. "I'd like your opinion on what we're looking at there. We could arrange a meeting at the station, after your normal hours at the cave, but this is quicker."

And quick was best. Particularly if her theory she hadn't shared with anyone yet was correct. Brooke nodded. "Let me go grab my work bag." She did so without running into Zeke, and that was best too. She doubted he was *unaware* of a police cruiser on his property, so he'd know where she'd gone. Or at least who with.

When she had everything she wanted, she returned to the car and slid into the front seat. Thomas immediately drove back out to the highway.

"I did put some feelers out on your father this morning," he offered. "Got some pretty straightforward answers. He's still in jail. There's no record of him getting out. He's not exactly a model prisoner. Lots of fights, solitary confinement, that sort of thing. I wouldn't anticipate him getting out anytime soon."

It should have been a relief but only left her with a deeper discomfort. Why did Royal think otherwise? Why did it still seem a threat lingered? But that wasn't Thomas's problem, so she wasn't about to lay it on him like it was.

"I really appreciate you looking into that for me," she said.

"Anytime." And he made it sound like nothing, which was kind of him. Like it didn't matter her father was a former Sons member, in jail for too many things to mention.

Further down the road, he pulled under the big archway that would lead them to the main house where most of the Hudson siblings lived and worked—both the ranch and their cold case investigation group, Hudson Sibling Solutions.

During the long winding drive, anxiety settled into her gut like a heavy weight. Thomas stopped in front of the grand ranch house. Brooke hesitated getting out of the car.

"I get that it feels…uncomfortable," Thomas said kindly. "I have to deliver a lot of bad news to people I know, people in my life. And so have the Hudsons. We all know how to divorce the messenger from the message."

Right. She nodded and got out of the car, following Thomas up the porch and waiting after he knocked on the door.

The woman who answered carried a tiny baby. She greeted them with a politeness and warmth that was antithetical to the situation. She ushered them into a big, cozy living room. Chloe was already there, sitting next to one of the Hudsons Brooke could remember by name. Jack Hudson was the sheriff of Sunrise, and the de facto leader of his siblings. He'd also been shot twice last month in the situation that had led to the discovery of human remains in the cave, causing her to stick around beyond just identifying the remains of his parents.

It wasn't obvious he'd been seriously hurt from just looking at him, but Brooke noted a cane in the corner next to the couch he sat on. And the careful way Chloe sat next to him.

"Chloe. Jack," Thomas greeted. "You remember Brooke Campbell, the forensic anthropologist."

Another woman entered. She didn't look like a Hudson, but a lot of significant others lived on the property, so Brooke assumed she was one of them.

"Brooke, this is Dahlia," Thomas introduced. "She's a librarian, but she has some archivist training. She's helping us keep the integrity of the scrapbook intact, like you suggested."

They exchanged pleasantries then everyone who was still standing sat down around a coffee table where Thomas placed the scrapbook with care. He opened up to a page in the middle. The pages were black, with black-and-white photos pasted in careful rows. He pointed to one such row.

"Doesn't this look like the preserve?" he asked everyone.

Jack and Chloe leaned forward and peered at the picture while Brooke did the same. She felt like an expert of the area around the cave now, but the photo wasn't very clear, and the black and white made it difficult to really determine. The picture could have been any rocky area with mountains in the distance.

Thomas slowly turned the page. "And these."

These pictures had two men in almost all of them. The prints weren't much clearer than the photo of the preserve, but it was obvious the subjects were in some kind of rock enclosure. It could definitely be a cave—but it could be their cave or any others.

"Aren't these pictures too old to use flashes or whatever in a dark cave?" Chloe asked. "Those guys look pretty old-timey."

"Yes, they do, but flash photography is pretty old," Dahlia replied. "Flashes have been around in some form or another for a long time, and there could have been other light sources involved outside the picture. There are photographs of caves over a hundred years old."

"Do you know who the subjects are?" Brooke asked. The surroundings didn't tell them much, but something about the two men drew her attention. She didn't know enough about historical fashion to know what era they were from, but certainly a long time ago.

"Let's see if we can remove the photo from the page. There might be a label on the back. Besides, we'll want to eventually remove all the pictures. The glue and paper used in these old scrapbooks are often harmful to photographs over time." Dahlia rummaged through her supplies, pulled out what resembled dental floss, and then carefully slid it under the upturned corner of the photo.

With a sawing motion, she pulled the floss through until the photo detached from the page.

She lifted the photo to the light, looked at the back. "The writing is faded, but it looks like it says 'F. Brink and L. Rogers.'"

Everyone turned to Chloe, whose father was a Brink and mother was Jen Rogers, the suspected murderer.

Chloe shook her head. "Far as I know, my grandpa Brink's name was George. Never met my mom's father. I always assumed he was dead or a deadbeat. But Rogers certainly explains my mother's connection to the scrapbook."

Brooke studied the picture. She didn't think anyone would assume the background of the black-and-white picture was a cave if they weren't currently dealing with a cave. But she could see what Thomas was talking about.

Certain formations surrounded the people were similar to the area she had just started excavating. Not irrevocable proof of the same cave, but maybe too much of a coincidence to not be.

"I could look into the family histories. See if these are direct ancestors of yours, Chloe. And if they are, it'd help us date the photograph. If you think it might help the case, Detective Hart."

Thomas frowned. "Not sure it'll help, but it can't hurt."

"This book adds to the case against Jen," Jack said. "She was living in that cave. She's the one who took the scrapbook from the police. Now you've found the scrapbook in there and there's a link to the Rogers family. Maybe it doesn't tell us anything new, but it can be used in the case against her."

Thomas nodded in agreement. "But why did she want to steal it then hide it?"

Brooke didn't have any answer for that question, but she kept studying the picture, trying to orient herself. Because caves changed over time, so it wasn't the same as now. But the formations were in the same spots, just different sizes.

And if she was seeing things correctly, and not jumping to conclusions, both men were standing next to each other in a corner of the cave she hadn't yet gotten to but knew made up the edge closest to the center of the cave. She'd purposefully left that spot for last because she'd wanted as much space around the interior studied and opened.

Maybe caves could appear similar, but there were too many coincidences here.

"Do you have a magnifying glass?" she asked absently to no one in particular. Some object at the men's feet looked like…*something.* Maybe if she could make it out, she could be sure one way or another.

Dahlia pulled a magnifying glass out of her supplies and handed it to Brooke. Brooke used it to analyze the lower corner of the bottom photograph. As the magnifying glass settled over the corner, the shape of something that looked like…hair and an ear. But the angle was all wrong. It was straight up and down, like it didn't have a body but had been propped there.

Brooke's heart started beating hard in her chest. She swallowed so her voice would sound calm. She held out the magnifying glass to Hart. "Is that a head?"

No one had been able to agree if the shape was a head. If the strands were hair, if the ear was indeed a human ear. They'd pored over the rest of the photos, searching for anything that might confirm what Brooke thought she saw.

No consensus could be made. Dahlia discussed some photo scanning and editing options to enhance the photos so the Hudsons were going to work on that angle. After all, if the pictures were that old, they might be dealing with a cold case—the Hudson Sibling Solutions specialty.

So, once they'd agreed on how to handle the photographs, Thomas had driven her to the cave. She'd jumped into work immediately, trying to focus on the place in the photograph. It was hard to pinpoint with the changes to the cave over time and from what little she had to go on.

Brooke wanted to dig with wild abandon. To see if she could find a skull right there. But she reminded herself to breathe, to take her time, to fall back on her training.

Finding answers relied on her ability to pay attention to every tiny detail. She couldn't rush just because they'd maybe discovered something.

So, hours went by, of careful, meticulous, slow-moving digging. She couldn't be haphazard. That wasn't her job. Her job was to unearth every last detail. Document them for study.

When she first came across a flash of bone in the cave fill, she nearly cried with relief. Her back muscles screamed, her eyes were gritty, and her hands were cramping. She was both somehow sweating from exertion and shivering from the cold air in the cave.

But she'd found something. So she focused her brainpower on the steps to carefully, correctly unearth whatever it was.

More time passed. She forgot Thomas was even there, and he never suggested they break for lunch, like he usually did. He just waited in silence and out of the way so she wouldn't concern herself with him or breaks.

Slowly, she uncovered what she'd hoped she'd find. A skull. In almost the exact place she might have seen a head in that picture. And just like in the photograph, the skull was buried with the jawbone down, top of the head up. There'd been some damage to the upper part of the skull. It just had to connect. It had to be the same. Skulls weren't buried like this.

She took a slow breath, reminding herself to remain calm. Reminding herself she was uncovering a mystery, not putting herself in danger.

"Thomas? Can you take some pictures?"

He walked over with his Bent County camera strapped around his neck. He looked at what she'd uncovered. He didn't outwardly react, but she knew he was feeling that same ticking clock she felt.

They were close to some kind of break in the case. So close. And if she could push through everything, they might have one.

"Just take as many photos as you can. I'm going to keep uncovering the skull."

So, that's what she set out to do. If she could remove the skull intact, with photo evidence of how it had been buried... She didn't know, but it was something.

Brooke lost track of anything but unearthing the skull, and once she could remove it from the cave floor and debris, she discovered exactly what she was afraid she might.

There was nothing directly underneath the skull. No bones from the neck or even shoulder that should be within the area she was excavating.

Just like the photograph.

"If that picture included a decapitated head, and this skull is that head, this death occurred before Jen Rogers,"

Thomas said, his voice devoid of any emotion, though she knew he felt something about that information whether he spoke it aloud or not.

Brooke looked up at Thomas and said what she'd been worried was true for a while.

"I think we're dealing with more than one killer."

Chapter Eleven

Zeke had thrown himself into his project after Brooke had taken off with Hart. He'd thought about figuring out *why* the detective had stopped by to pick her up, but it was none of his business.

Maybe putting together a makeshift lab on his ranch wasn't either, particularly with the stalking threat no longer an issue.

But even if he believed that Royal had done jail time for *maybe* a justified crime, the man was a potential threat. There were still *threats* around Brooke and what she was doing. Zeke couldn't just accept that she wasn't in *some* danger.

And he didn't think she'd accepted that, even if she'd pretended to. Because her things were still in his house. She hadn't told him to jump off a cliff...yet.

Worse, he couldn't even blame her. He owed her an apology, and that burned. He shouldn't have kissed her. He shouldn't have *touched* her. And he could not for the life of him figure out why his usual iron-tight control had deserted him when it came to her.

He studied his work on the makeshift lab. Only some of the equipment Granger had set him up with had been delivered, but the barn was sparkling clean and what he'd managed to get in terms of tables and whatnot had been set up.

He glanced at his watch and ignored the fact it was later than usual and Brooke hadn't returned yet.

He wouldn't read into that. He wouldn't *worry*. Hart knew where she was staying. If something bad had happened, he'd have heard by now.

That became a mantra as evening turned into straight-up nighttime, and he stopped being able to distract himself with work. So he'd ended up sitting on the chair that looked out the front window, waiting for Viola to sound the alarm or headlights to appear.

It was nearing midnight when Viola let out a bark and Zeke saw the Bent County cruiser finally drop her off. He was wound so tight, he couldn't even fully feel relief.

She stepped into the living room, creeping quietly. She looked bedraggled and tired, which was none of his business. None of his concern.

Yet all these things he kept telling himself weren't his business or concern took up residence inside him. And that stupid kiss this morning had illuminated why.

Zeke was not a man who believed in love that didn't come from family and trauma ties. There was nothing romantic about the hell of a world he'd born into.

But he didn't know what else to call what he'd felt for Brooke all those years ago, and how much those feelings he didn't understand, didn't like, didn't *want*, still existed within him.

Once she closed and locked the door behind her, she turned and crouched to pet an excited Viola. When her gaze lifted, she jumped a little at the sight of him sitting on the chair.

Brooke cleared her throat and straightened. "You didn't have to wait up."

He snorted. Like he would have been able to sleep. "Why'd you work so late?" He'd *promised* himself he wouldn't ask.

She looked at him a little quizzically but took the question in stride as she dropped her bag and then walked over to the couch and sank into it. Viola hopped up next to her. "Break in the case, sort of. Didn't want to stop until I'd gotten something accomplished." She leaned her head on the back of the couch, closing her eyes. "I don't suppose you'd be up to making me dinner?"

The fact she was asking anything of him—kiss or no— was concerning. So was the way she could just completely forget that kiss this morning. Still, he got to his feet. "You must be starving if you're asking me to do something for you."

She gave him the ghost of a smile. "I haven't eaten since… I actually don't remember. We found something, I guess. It felt like nothing and something all at the same time."

"I know how that goes. You relax. I'll fix up something for you to eat." He moved into the kitchen, grateful for something to do when everything was whirling inside of him like some kind of storm. Like this morning. Out of control.

And he couldn't allow that. Certainly couldn't grab her and kiss her again when she was running on fumes. *Or at all*, he told himself sternly.

He could throw a frozen pizza in the oven, but he poked around his pantry instead, frustrated with himself for wanting to fuss over her when he didn't *fuss*. The only place he even acknowledged that impulse was with his family and he'd never had to act on it. Fussing had always been Walker's job.

That was why the best Zeke could come up with was a can of stew and some buttered bread and a couple pieces of cheese. It was hardly the stuff of homemade meals, but it was warm and hearty, and hopefully comforting.

He went to tell her it was ready, but when he stepped into the living room, her head was still resting against the back of the couch, her eyes were closed, her breathing even. Exhausted, clearly.

He wanted to bundle her up in a bed and let her sleep for at least a day. But then she blinked her eyes open, gaze meeting his like a vise around his chest. Squeezing until he popped.

"Food's ready," he managed to roughly rasp. "But you can sleep."

She pushed herself off the couch, looking away from him. "If I let myself go to sleep without eating, I'll regret it. Learned that one the hard way." She walked into the dining room, settled herself at the table, made a contented noise at the view of the food or at Viola settling herself on Brooke's feet.

"Thanks for this. I owe you one."

He nodded with a jerk, so uncomfortable he could hardly stand it. *No one* made him uncomfortable. He didn't let them.

Case in point, he was going to apologize for this morning, because he'd been out of line. He'd been wrong. To be mad at her. To take it out on her. To *kiss* her...even if she'd kissed him back.

He wasn't fazed by his mistakes. He didn't marinate in them. No, sir. He dealt. He'd made a mistake, now he'd apologize for it.

"I'm sorry."

She didn't look at him at first. Her gaze remained on her bowl before she brought a spoonful of stew to her mouth and chewed thoughtfully. "Sorry for what?" she asked after too many beats of silence.

Zeke didn't scowl, though he wanted to. Because she knew *for what*. There was only one thing to be sorry for. Besides, he could tell by the expression on her face she wasn't confused—he knew her too well. She wanted to make him say it.

Well, he wasn't *ashamed*. He was sorry. So… "For kissing you the way that I did. At an inappropriate time and moment."

She seemed to mull that over but said nothing else. That was fine. They didn't need to have a conversation about it. The point was the apology. Not coming to some kind of consensus about what was over and done.

He moved to wash out the pan he'd heated her stew in. He'd tidy up the kitchen and go to bed, like she should. He wasn't going to say another damn thing.

But had she not understood? He'd always thought she had. Wasn't that why she'd scared the hell out of him? She'd seen through him, too easily. And now she was just…sitting there, like his apology or the kiss or *something* didn't mean anything.

She had kissed him back. She had not pushed him away. He'd been the one to end it. So there was *something*, and didn't they both deserve to go over that *something*, so somewhere along the line they could move on and all *this* wouldn't whirl between them?

"Did I ever tell you why I joined North Star?" he demanded. When he *knew* this wasn't the way around what he was feeling. Because he was angry again, this big, huge *thing* inside him taking over. No control. No finesse.

"You wanted to help people like your family," she said, not quite meeting his gaze. "Your cousin was already in North Star and she brought you in after your stint in the army."

He shook his head. Even if he was surprised at how many details she'd retained, it wasn't the real story. Maybe back then he'd told her it was. Maybe he'd even convinced himself it was when he'd been young and in so much denial it should have choked him.

It was hard to look back with a critical eye and know where exactly he'd started to change, mature, evolve. He only knew that, standing in the kitchen of a ranch he'd bought and begun to rebuild, he was different than he had been.

"Yeah, Mallory got me into North Star because our dads were worthless Sons's pawns and I had some military training. But the real reason I joined the army, joined North Star, was because I couldn't *deal*."

Her eyebrows drew together, clearly not understanding what he meant. And he wasn't even sure what he meant. Just all of these…things rambling around inside him, grappling for purchase. He couldn't seem to put them away, any more than the words.

Zeke had never admitted that out loud. Never let himself poke into that old feeling. But here it was, and he didn't know why he thought it a good idea to lay it at her feet, but that's what he was doing.

And he couldn't stop.

"I couldn't hold it together. Every moment since my mother was murdered when I was a teenager, I felt like I was on this edge, ready to explode, because everything mattered too much. Keeping Carlyle safe, figuring out who killed our mother, helping Walker keep us together. It was too much. I couldn't *take* it. But the army? North Star? I could do that, and…well, because they weren't my family. Because they weren't the people I loved. I could set all the feelings aside and do what needed to be done."

When he met her gaze, it was shocked and on his, the piece of cheese in her hand clearly forgotten since she didn't bring it to her mouth. He felt like he'd run a marathon. It was hard to breathe. It was hard to…

Everything was just *hard* because she was sitting at his kitchen table, as pretty as the day he'd met her, even though she was run ragged. And what did it say about him that he was having this conversation with her when she was exhausted and hungry?

But she was in his kitchen, and the past four years had disappeared because she'd never been off his mind. He'd ended things, and he'd been living with a heavy, ignored regret ever since. Keeping it buried underneath *action*— North Star cases, then helping Walker track down their mother's murderer. And for the past few months, he'd had nothing to do except deal with the fact that he was almost thirty years old and likely still had a hell of a lot of life left to live.

With no missions on the horizon. Just all that *life*.

He hadn't wanted to miss her, hadn't wanted to wish she was somehow present when he'd had this realization life existed beyond a death wish.

But he had missed her. The whole time, and now she was here and…in danger. *Danger.*

"So it's like that all over again," he continued, because apparently once he started spouting all this, he couldn't contain the rest. And maybe something could ease if she understood. How hard this was. How much she meant. "This untenable pressure. The thought of anything happening to you is more than I can bear. You matter too much."

She blinked at him once before returning her gaze back to her bowl. "Maybe we shouldn't talk about this," she said quietly.

"That's fine." And he meant it. He wasn't interested in a walk down memory lane. Or he thought he wasn't. But he was the one who'd started all this. He could have let her eat and go to sleep. He could have said he was sorry and left it at that. He was the one pushing.

He didn't *need* to push, not if she didn't want to. This wasn't four years ago. He could give her feelings, her *wants*, the space they needed. Even if they weren't him.

Seemed about the way things usually went anyway.

He finished cleaning the kitchen and then noticed she'd eaten most of her food. She handed him her dishes and he washed them. She dried them in a quiet, easy show of teamwork.

So much about them wasn't easy but working together always had been.

She gave him the dried dishes so he could put them away. Then she turned from him, no doubt to go upstairs and go to sleep. She clearly needed a really good night's sleep. Hopefully she wouldn't wake up at the crack of dawn to sneak out tomorrow morning like she had this morning.

She paused before stepping out of his visibility. When she spoke, it was quiet but so damn sure every word landed like a stab wound. He'd had a few of those, so he knew.

"You didn't love me, Zeke."

He inhaled sharply. "You really don't think I was in love with you?" He stared at the back of her head, at the careful way she held herself. He really hadn't thought she could *hurt* him quite that viscerally. How could she have gone through what they'd been to each other and think that?

"You said you weren't."

That, he *knew* he'd never said. He'd never used the word *love*. *Ever.* "No, I said I didn't see a future. Because I didn't. A future meant having…hope. It meant caring more about survival than anything else. And you said it yourself back then. I had a death wish. Danger didn't faze me because if I didn't make it out, oh well."

She turned to face him and there was no shock on her face. Those were words she'd said *to* him all those years ago. She'd known, even then, he hadn't valued his life that much. But he wasn't sure he'd ever shared all the *why* behind it with her.

So when she didn't speak, that's what he did. Like this was some kind of confession and the dark feelings he kept locked down had to come out for him to be saved. Absolved.

"I used to think that if I died doing something honorable, my siblings would be proud," he said while she looked at him with heartbreak in her eyes. "It took… maturity, I guess, to realize they'd just blame themselves." He wasn't even sure when that realization had happened. Maybe when he'd been shot in the showdown that had taken down their mother's murderer. The way Carlyle had lost it. The way Walker had babied him afterward.

The way the Hudsons had somehow absorbed them into their world just because Mary had fallen in love with Walker. Or maybe, more importantly, because Walker had fallen head over drooling heels for Mary.

"Well, I'm glad you realized that," she said, her voice sounding strangled.

"Me too." He wasn't sure he had been, until this moment. Glad maybe not for himself, but for the people he cared about.

She nodded carefully, like she was afraid she might shatter if she moved too quickly. "Good night, Zeke."

"Night." And only after she left, the dog padding behind her, did he realize he'd been hoping for a different outcome. Because he could tell himself the old reasons for not wanting her in his life...

But they just weren't true anymore.

BROOKE OPENED HER eyes to sunlight streaming in through the window. It was later than she should have let herself sleep, but her head had hit the pillow last night and she'd been *out*.

No energy to work through everything Zeke had told her. The way he'd looked at her. But it was the first thing on her mind this morning, even groggy and still tired.

You really don't think I was in love with you?

He'd sounded so shocked, and worse, hurt. And maybe he was right. Maybe he'd never told her he hadn't loved her, but he'd never told her he *had*. Then he'd broken it off with her because there'd been no future. Was she really supposed to believe that had been love on his part?

She'd found an entire skull yesterday with no other bones in the immediate vicinity. She needed to get to the police station and process it and send it down to Cheyenne. She needed to check on her lab results for the last set of bones and write up a report for Thomas so he could take the multiple murderer theory to the rest of his investigative team.

She could not lie in this comfortable bed and think about Zeke loving her. Or that kiss yesterday morning that already felt like a month ago.

But for just a *few* more minutes, she let last night's conversation replay in her head. She'd had her own terrible childhood with parents who hadn't cared, and the hell of being separated from Royal and bouncing around foster houses as a teen, but Zeke's story of his mother's murder had always struck her as more sad.

He'd loved his mother and lost her in tragedy. No hope there. She'd only ever loved Royal, and she hadn't really lost him. Maybe their separation had been hard, but she'd always had hope for a future where they were together again.

In fact, at the moment, her brother was another item on her to-do list, because she had to tell him that their father was still in jail, so whatever he thought was happening…wasn't.

Probably.

She shook it away. One step at a time, and work had to come first right now. So she took a shower, got dressed for the day, and typed a to-do list into her phone to help her feel somehow in charge of the overwhelming amount of tasks she had to accomplish.

When she went downstairs, Viola greeted her with a wagging tail and happy yips at the bottom of the stairs. Brooke smelled coffee and bacon. For a moment, she stood and felt a pang.

One she didn't have time to dissect.

When she stepped into the kitchen, Zeke was putting two plates piled high with eggs, bacon and biscuits on the table.

"You don't have to keep cooking for me, Zeke," she

said because it settled in her chest like a heavy weight. Why was he doing things for her all the time? "I am capable of feeding myself."

"Sure," he replied easily. "But isn't it nice to have someone else handle it? You're busy, Brooke. I'm not. I can handle a few chores. Besides, last night wasn't much. I'm not much of a dinner cook, but I can put together a mean breakfast." He gestured to the table. "Sit. Eat."

She looked at the table, hesitating. Because she was afraid she'd…get used to this. Someone taking care of her. Because she'd never once had that.

Except when she was with him.

But she wasn't *with* him. He was just acting as… bodyguard. Maybe there'd been some personal conversations. A kiss. That was just…sorting out a past. When she walked off this ranch, it wouldn't be like him breaking up with her all over again.

She couldn't let it be.

"Hart called," Zeke said. "He had court this morning, so couldn't be out at the cave, and Laurel's still out. He said he could send another deputy out with you, but he'd prefer from here on out it just be the detectives if you didn't mind taking the morning off from excavating."

She wasn't sure why the detective had shared that information with Zeke rather than leave her a message or text on her own phone, but didn't know if she wanted to dig too deep into anything that involved Zeke at the moment.

So she sat and ate breakfast next to him. She didn't say anything. She really didn't know what to say, and he seemed to be in the same boat. The only sounds in the kitchen were the scraping of forks and the dog occasionally huffing at their feet.

They even washed the dishes in silence. But once they were done and before she could excuse herself, Zeke opened the back door from the kitchen.

"I want to show you something, if you're up for a little walk?"

She hesitated. He wasn't exactly…acting like himself, but she couldn't sort out what that meant. He was more calm than he'd been yesterday, but there was a kind of grimness wrapped into it that she didn't know how to parse.

"Okay."

They both got shoes on and then she followed him out into the sunny late morning. Viola dashed into the yard, then dashed back, over and over again, making Brooke smile as they walked to a building. A barn, she supposed.

Zeke stopped at a normal-size door on the side of the barn, pulled a key out from his pocket, and unlocked it. Then he held the key out to her.

She frowned.

"It's yours," he said, pushing the key into her palm. Then he shoved the door open and gestured her inside.

She stepped into a darkened barn, though it didn't *smell* like a barn. It smelled…clean. And when lights flipped on above her, she realized why. This was no barn to house horses or store crops. It looked like…a lab. Her old lab at North Star, to be precise.

"Is this…?" She stepped forward then stopped herself and looked back at him.

"It's a private lab. To run whatever tests. Granger helped with the supplies, information to make sure everything is up to code, just like you used to have at North Star. So it should be most of what you need, but he can get us anything else. A few things he sent need to arrive yet, but we'll get there."

Brooke felt frozen in place. It was set up perfectly. Not *quite* like any of the labs she'd worked with at different police organizations, but that's because they were often multipurpose, underfunded and overcrowded.

Her North Star lab had been different—set up exactly the way she liked—because they hadn't exactly always been working within the law. "I'm not sure anything I do here would hold up in court."

That was a very ungrateful thing to say. When he'd gone to all this trouble. When he'd reached out to Granger. When she could test that skull here *immediately*.

Zeke shrugged and didn't voice any irritation with her response, even though he had every right to. "You don't have to use it. Or you can use it in conjunction with the lab in Cheyenne. Up to you."

Up to her. But that was ridiculous. This whole thing was so damn ridiculous. "Why did you do this?"

"Because I was worried the lab in Cheyenne and the sheer amount of people dealing with your case might have something to do with what was going on with you being followed. So, I got the ball rolling with Granger, and then it just felt like you might as well have some space here to work. You've got a lot of remains to work through."

Didn't she just.

And because her heart seemed too big for her chest, and her eyes were full of tears she wasn't about to let fall, she changed the subject entirely.

"How is Granger?" she asked, inspecting one of the machines. She would have thought he'd gotten rid of all this once North Star had disbanded. She should have known Granger MacMillan might have let North Star the entity go, but he wasn't about to not have the means to help anyone who needed it.

"Looks like him and Shay are swamped in foster kids and farm animals."

Brooke smiled. She hadn't talked to her old North Star bosses in a while. She hated to bother them when they had this new life they were building.

"Do you keep in touch with anyone else?"

"Oh, sure. Here and there. You don't?"

She didn't want to answer that. So many of her old North Star friends she'd retreated from. Because they'd all been starting new lives, and she didn't want to be some old reminder, some old burden. So she'd just…held herself apart. She'd never refused a call, but she hadn't made any. She'd kept to herself.

It was a bit of a surprise Zeke hadn't. Zeke who had provided this… It was really too much. To think about the two people who'd run North Star, who'd taken down the Sons and saved so many people, now married and raising kids and farm animals and just living a normal kind of life… While she was standing here with Zeke.

All she'd ever wanted and known she couldn't have.

That, she just couldn't deal with right now. Old feelings. Mixed-up nostalgia and dreams and delusion.

So she turned to Zeke. The emotional stuff didn't matter, did it? She had a case to solve. And now she had some things she could do right here. Everything else he'd said last night didn't matter, even if deep down she wanted it to.

They'd had their chance. It hadn't worked. She had bigger things to concern herself with right now.

So she smiled at him, and focused on work. "Want to help me smuggle a skull?"

His mouth quirked. "You know me so well."

Chapter Twelve

Zeke waited for Brooke to gather her stuff, and then he drove her into Bent and the sheriff's department. She instructed him not to follow her inside. He was supposed to drive around, get some coffee or something, then come back at one and pick her up.

Her idea, and while he didn't like taking orders from anyone, he found he didn't mind Brooke being in charge. Besides, staying away was easier than trying to explain his presence to the deputies and detectives inside. He would likely raise a few eyebrows and questions that might make it more difficult for Brooke to do what she'd gone there to do.

He was still having a hard time believing she was going to essentially steal remains. Maybe she'd been trained in the North Star way of bending the rules that needed bending, but he'd certainly never seen her bend any rule with ruthless efficiency.

She wanted to be good, always, because the thing about Brooke Campbell was, no matter how she'd grown up, no matter how much time she'd spent in North Star, she was good down to her soul.

Still, she spent her days studying the remains of dead people. That had really never computed with her personality, either, and yet she did it, and well. Analyzed that grue-some data and put it together in even more grim reports.

Still she managed to be soft and lovely and *her*.

Zeke sighed and tried not to wonder if he'd never seen her again, would he have gone through life in denial of what was missing from it?

He returned to the station a little before the appointed time and just stood outside his truck, watching the com-ings and goings of a county police force.

He'd considered going to the police academy the past few months. He needed something to do, and he kept re-sisting the idea of actually trying to ranch. It left a hell of a lot of room for failure.

Police work? He could do that. Well... Following rules and laws had never been in his wheelhouse, even when he'd been in the army. He liked to do things *his* way. But he knew how to deal with people, with clear rules and expectations.

Sort of.

He could have joined the Hudsons like Walker had done. The HSS had invited him to become an investiga-tor. Mostly he'd declined because being around all that family, marriages, babies, *life* made him more itchy than he cared to analyze.

He could have done lots of things. Gone lots of places.

And instead he'd stayed in Sunrise and bought a *ranch*.

It hit him at the oddest times that these past few months had been the calmest of his life and the most uncomfort-able and unsettled he'd ever felt. And still, with all that internal upheaval, he hadn't bolted. Because with Walker and Carlyle safe and happy and settling down, it didn't feel right to leave them behind to worry about him.

Luckily he didn't have to consider that any longer because Brooke walked out of the police station, her hands gripping the straps of her backpack. No doubt because she'd succeeded and there was a skull in there. Her grip was all nerves.

But she walked slowly and calmly to him, the sunlight dancing in the reddish strands of her hair. And there was that vise around his chest again, like a full breath would break him to pieces.

Like *she* would.

She got into his truck without looking at him, placing the backpack in the backseat with care.

He got into the driver's seat, trying to focus on the problem at hand over his pointless, roundabout thoughts. She needed to take the remains back to the ranch and work in her lab.

But he had other ideas. "I was thinking we should pick your car up on the way back to my ranch. Keep moving it around. Just to be safe."

"But Royal was the one following me. I mean I'm all for having my car back, but we have that," she said, nodding at her backpack.

Mostly he agreed with her. He'd even tossed the tracker he'd put on his truck the other morning because he was fairly certain Royal had been the one to put it on Brooke's car. He had been the one following her, so nothing else added up.

But…

"I'll just drop you off at your car. *That* can ride with me from the cabin to ranch," he said, jerking his chin toward the backpack. "I'll follow you and make sure we're in eyesight of each other."

She didn't look convinced that this was the best idea, but she didn't argue, so he drove to the rental cabin. It wasn't that far out of their way, and she should have her vehicle. Even if he didn't like the idea of her having the means to leave without him watching out for her.

Royal had been following her though, and she still might be in danger, but until Zeke figured out what *kind*, leaving her car at the rental just gave Royal the means to cause more trouble.

Zeke pulled up next to her car, not bothering to turn off the engine. She scrambled out of his truck with one last glance at her backpack, then pulled keys out of her purse and headed to the car.

It was fine. She'd lead the way and he'd follow in his truck. What bad could happen? They'd still be together, and they'd head for his ranch.

But before, in that diner parking lot, there'd been a tracker. He was pretty sure it had been Royal, but something in his mind whispered, *What if it's not?*

"Wait." He hopped out of the truck and began to inspect her car just as he had back at the diner days ago. Maybe he was paranoid, but he'd built most of his adult life on following instincts a lot of people called paranoia. Sometimes it was and sometimes…

"Do you smell that?"

Brooke frowned, sniffed the air. "I don't know. Maybe? It just smells like…fertilizer."

And maybe it was, but something buzzed along Zeke's skin. A bad feeling that he'd honed from being in a lot of close calls in his life. He took Brooke's arm and drew her away from the vehicle. "Look, I think—"

The sound of the explosion was small, but still a surprise. Brooke jumped and Zeke tried to shelter her. When he looked back at the car, flames erupted from under the hood. Zeke grabbed Brooke and pulled her behind him, propelling them both back and away from the fire.

It hadn't been anything major. Unlikely to kill anyone, though it could have easily hurt someone near the car. There might be a second explosion if the fire hit the gas tank, so they needed to get some distance from it.

"Did it...overheat?" Brooke asked weakly when it was obvious that's not what had happened.

The door of the cabin burst open and Royal, in his bare feet, ran out holding a fire extinguisher. For a second he stared at the blaze then turned to them.

"You okay, Brooke?"

"Yes," she said firmly, but she was shaking underneath Zeke's hand.

Royal moved forward and put out the fire with quick, efficient movements. Then he shoved his free hand over his short hair. "What the hell was that?"

"We don't know." Zeke surveyed the car, Royal, and Brooke behind him. He sighed, because whatever was going on wasn't over. And it wasn't just about Brooke.

"Get some shoes on, Royal. You're coming with us."

BROOKE WAS STILL SHAKING, but could breathe with more ease when Zeke's ranch came into view. Nothing bad had happened here. They were safe here. Everyone was going to be safe.

She had to believe that. So she'd repeated it over and over inside her head on the drive.

She was surprised Royal hadn't mounted a fight about coming to Zeke's. He'd simply gone inside, gotten shoes and a duffel bag, and returned. Zeke had helped her into the truck and handed her the backpack so she could hold on to it. Royal had climbed in the back.

She was riding in a truck, clutching a skull carefully packaged in a backpack, her brother in the back seat while her ex pulled up to his ranch house. After her car had… exploded. Kind of.

It was a small *explosion*, she kept telling herself. Nothing compared to some of the things she'd seen in North Star. And still, it had shaken her more because it had been *her* car. In front of *her* rental cabin, even if she hadn't been staying there.

She didn't know *why*, but this somehow felt centered on *her*. And worse, it probably wasn't about the skeletal remains at all, because she'd been working on those for over a month now. Nothing had changed this week—not really.

Except Royal's appearance in her life. So maybe it didn't center on her at all. She didn't want to feel this way, but she couldn't help but think it focused on Royal. It had to. Nothing bad had been happening to her or around her until he'd started following her.

When Zeke shoved the truck into Park, they all got out. Viola bounded over, a low growl in her throat as she scurried up to Royal. It was a warning, but also clearly curiosity on the dog's part.

Royal crouched, holding out his hand in supplication to the dog. Viola sniffed, tail stuck straight out, but after a few seconds, it began to wag and the dog let Royal scratch her ears. Royal grinned up at Brooke over the dog. For a moment, they were kids again and she hadn't failed her brother and they weren't in trouble.

"Someone will call that in before nightfall," Zeke said, interrupting her little moment with pesky *facts*. "Someone involved with the rentals will see there's been a fire in that car and will call *someone* about it. Then Bent County is going to know it's your car that got torched, Brooke. If we aren't the ones to call it in, it looks fishy," Zeke said.

"It *is* fishy," Royal muttered irritably as he straightened into a standing position.

"Yeah. Do you want Bent County looking into it?" Zeke asked somewhat pointedly. Like Royal might have a reason to hide. And he might. He probably did. He…

Royal looked over at her. "Did you tell him?"

"Tell me what?" Zeke demanded, his eyebrows drawing together.

But Brooke ignored Zeke. She had to, or she might just…fall apart. And there was too much at stake. She had to get to work on this skull. She had to date it. She had…things to do that weren't *this*.

First, Royal needed to know. "Dad is still in jail," she said to Royal and only to Royal. "Whatever you think he's cooked up isn't true. I had it confirmed yesterday."

Royal frowned, not looking convinced.

"What do you think he's cooked up?" Zeke asked.

"I don't know," Royal said, scowling. "That's the problem."

"And you didn't think that you might mention to me that your father might be the issue here?" Zeke said to her. *Oh* so calmly.

"No, because I confirmed with Thomas that he's still in jail." She lifted her chin, met his calm expression, but saw the anger in his eyes. "So he's *not* the problem." And it just broke whatever last piece of control or something she had within her, because she was just done. With both of them.

"Because you see, Zeke, I've been taking care of myself and my life for the past four years. Without *you*. I appreciate the place to stay. I even appreciate the interference, up to a point, but I won't be made to feel guilty for taking care of myself."

He didn't say anything in response, but there was that old stony expression on his face she remembered all too well. She turned to her brother. "I didn't have any problems with anyone until you started following me. Are you sure this isn't a *you* problem?"

"You think I just lured people here to set your car on fire?" he returned, a lot of belligerence covering up a hurt.

She felt guilty and knew she shouldn't. So she just… let it all out. "I don't know what to think. But I do know I sent you letters, supplied an attorney, did everything I could with the resources I had to find you, to help you, and I never heard a *peep*. And you've waltzed back into my life and suddenly there's danger, and you're giving me attitude. Frankly, I'm sick of both of you. I'm taking my skull and I'm getting some work done."

And that's just what she did. She took the backpack and marched over toward the barn, Viola at her heels. She unlocked the door then carefully knelt down to pet Viola.

"I'm sorry. No dogs allowed in the lab. And I'm about to institute a no men rule too. Maybe you could be my guard dog and keep them out."

With that, she slid inside the barn, keeping Viola out. She hung the backpack up on a hook and then went to the sink to wash her hands. Everything was in working order. Just like her other labs.

She didn't think about Zeke doing that for her. She didn't think about her brother, or her brother and Zeke together. She focused on her *work*.

Because that was the only thing she'd ever been able to depend on. Human remains might be a mystery, but they were a set of data points. Not infuriating, obnoxious, changeable *people*.

Not people who expected you to rely on them, to trust them, to tell them the truth, but didn't extend the same courtesy. Not people you let yourself depend on a *little*, who then disappeared.

Because you're too much of a bother, Brooke. Best keep to yourself.

Since she wanted to cry, she carefully got everything ready, unpacked her skull, then got to work. Right now, her goal was to date the bones as best she could, particularly in relation to the other remains they'd found. So far, they'd uncovered mostly intact bodies. So this was new. It was different. It needed studying.

She didn't know how long she worked. She left her phone off. If Thomas wanted to contact her about the cave…well, he'd have to hunt her down. When the door to the lab opened however many hours later, she saw it was dark out.

She blinked. A whole day in here. She'd gotten a lot done and no one had bothered her. Not even to get her to eat.

Somehow most of the mad she'd had at Zeke was gone. He'd done all this for her, and it wasn't his fault… None of this was about him, but here he was.

"Any progress?" he asked. No bringing up earlier. No being cold to her. Just a genuine question.

So she gave a genuine answer. "Some. I think this skull is fairly old. It's also the only bone we've found that didn't have an intact body with or nearby it. And I can't help but think it matches a picture from that scrapbook Thomas uncovered."

Zeke nodded. "That's good progress, right?"

"It is."

He stood in silence as she cleaned up for the day. She needed something to eat, to stretch out her back. She needed… Oh, she didn't know.

"Brooke, I put this lab together, helped you get that skull, because I thought the stalking might be connected to the case, but now I wonder…"

Probably the same thing she did. "If they're wholly unrelated?"

Zeke nodded. "Royal and I talked, and he agrees. He didn't know anything about what you were doing here. When I explained you had a real human skull in your backpack, I think his opinion of you changed entirely. He was very perplexed."

She wanted to laugh. She really did. But on the other side of her temper was always that awful guilt. And she knew what it stemmed from. You didn't grow up in a gang and then get bounced around to foster homes without developing a certain amount of trauma responses. She didn't want to be a bother, didn't want to hurt anyone in case they might ditch her.

But he already had ditched her, so to speak. And still, she couldn't resist the apology. "I'm sorry I didn't tell you Royal's theory about our father trying to…do something."

"I thought you wouldn't be made to feel guilty about not including me in something that was none of my business?"

This time she did laugh in spite of herself. He recited her words with such dry disdain it was just *funny.* "I tried. But I'm really good at feeling guilty. And the truth is, if you were anyone else, I probably would have told you. I'd probably be more comfortable involving you and asking you for help. But it's…you."

"What about me?" he returned, eyebrows furrowed. Clearly confused, even if she thought he shouldn't be. "I've helped you lots."

"Yes. You have. In a North Star capacity. But not after. Zeke, I was so desperately in love with you then. I didn't hide that. Surely you know that."

She wouldn't say he looked *uncomfortable* with her saying those things, but he certainly wasn't going to interact with the idea of *love*, even after he'd said all that stuff last night. For whatever reasons, and maybe they were *good* reasons, he didn't want to deal with the idea of love. Then or now.

Still, maybe it was her turn to try to explain herself. Because he wasn't doing it to be cruel. He'd never really been cruel to her. She knew what that was like.

"Those are not just feelings that go away, and it took me a long time to…resituate myself once we broke up, once North Star ended. I don't want to ever have to go through that kind of…upheaval again. I have been bounced around at other people's whims my *entire life*. Finally, I have some…some agency. Some power. I can't just hand it over because maybe something dangerous is going on. I can't lose myself again. I have to stand on my own two feet."

He was silent a moment and then nodded. "Okay."

She blinked once. His easy agreement was the last thing she'd expected. She'd braced for a lecture about protection not being the opposite of agency and so on and so forth. She'd heard something of the like in North Star her entire time there. She narrowed her eyes at him. She did not trust Zeke Daniels's calm acquiescence. "What do you mean 'okay'?"

"I mean okay. That sounds fair and right, and the last thing I want to do is hurt you again. But I also want you to consider that I don't swoop in because…I'm trying to inflict my whims on you. I'm trying to keep you safe, not keep you from standing up for yourself too. In fact, I'd like all four of us to work together to make that happen."

Help was not the enemy. Brooke knew that from an investigative standpoint, but she was still trying to accept it on a personal, adult level. She'd always done everything on her own there. But she couldn't handle whatever this was on her own, and she knew it. So why couldn't she accept help from someone she trusted, even if he'd broken her heart?

Even if, worse, she still had feelings for him and was afraid it would lead her down the same heartbroken path?

Regardless, she had to set those feelings aside and be reasonable. "I'd like that too." She frowned. "But who's the fourth person?"

"Hart. He came by looking for you so you could excavate. I haven't told him everything, and God knows Royal hasn't told us much, but between the four of us… Maybe we can get to the bottom of everything."

Everything. She wasn't sure it was possible, but she supposed now was the time to try.

Chapter Thirteen

They convened in the living room. The afternoon had been…tense at best, but Zeke was hopeful they'd all come to a kind of understanding about the most important thing. Figuring out what was going on so they could keep Brooke safe.

The men in the group made quite a trio. The cop, the con and whatever Zeke was. Some combination of the two, he supposed.

Then there was Brooke. She'd let go of her mad. She always did. Too quickly, in Zeke's estimation, but he couldn't be frustrated with her over it in the current situation. Not when her *I was so desperately in love with you* would echo in his head for the rest of his life.

Both the way she'd said it, so serious and with all that emotion, that hurt *he'd* inflicted just there in her eyes. And then the past tense she'd used. Lov*ed*. Yeah, he found he didn't care for that.

"We dusted your car for prints," Thomas was saying to Brooke. "We're running what we found through our system, but I can't imagine we come back with anything. It was a small very-homemade bomb. Very hard to trace. There was some thought put behind that."

"I think the bigger concern is that we don't know what

the hell the point of it was," Zeke pointed out. He'd thrown some frozen pizzas in the oven and they were now eating them over the coffee table in the living room since his kitchen table couldn't hold four people comfortably.

Viola moved from person to person, begging for scraps. It might have been homey. Four friends enjoying a meal.

Instead they were discussing car bombs and murder.

"It wouldn't have really hurt anyone," Royal said. "Not unless someone had the hood open when the bomb went off. Even then, not lethal. Maybe just some burns. So the point had to be to scare, not necessarily to accomplish any injury."

"Scare who, I wonder," Brooke said quietly. Her gaze was on her brother. "Me, because it's my car?"

That, Zeke figured, had been everyone's initial thought.

"Or you, Royal, because you were at the rental?" she questioned.

Royal's expression went even more grim. "Not a soul knows I'm here."

"Did you check *your* car for a tracking device?" Zeke asked. Because even if this somehow connected to Brooke's work, who would just…scare her like that? Without some kind of direct threat, there was no reason to know who or what was behind what was happening. No way to react any way when you didn't know *why* you were being scared.

For a moment, Royal's face registered some surprise. "Well. No." He got to his feet. "I'll go look right now."

Brooke stood. "I'll drive you."

"Brooke."

Zeke tried not to grimace at the fact he and Hart had said her name at the same time.

"He shouldn't go alone," Brooke said, stubbornly to Zeke's mind.

"I'll go with him," Hart said, pushing to his feet to stand next to Royal. "We'll take the cruiser. Check in with where the deputies are at on the investigation while we're there."

Brooke frowned, but she didn't mount an argument. And to Zeke's surprise, neither did Royal. Zeke supposed he'd have to count it as a point in Royal's favor that he was willing to head out with a cop. Another point in his favor was that he'd been willing to consider Zeke's suggestion in the first place.

"I'll drop Royal back here after we're done. If we find a tracker, we'll look at it from a law-enforcement angle this time." Hart eyed them all with a kind of censure. As if they should have come to him in the first place.

"And I'll let Laurel in on everything," he continued. "More eyes until we get a clearer perspective on what this is. But you'll need to get back to the caves tomorrow, Brooke. We've got to determine if we're looking for another murderer there. We have to treat this as two concurrent cases we're working on. Not one or the other."

Zeke could read the guilt all over Brooke's face. No doubt because she had a skull at her lab here on his property and she hadn't told either of the detectives she'd smuggled it out of the station.

Zeke would have to give *her* a point for still not saying anything. He knew it went against her rule-following nature.

Royal and Hart departed and then Brooke and Zeke were left together. She got up and began to clean the remnants of pizza, so Zeke did the same. She didn't say anything. She was quiet and withdrawn and he just...hated it.

"It's totally possible this thing doesn't connect to you,

Brooke," he offered, hoping to get that tenseness out of her shoulders.

"It was still my car they were tracking. And bombed. Maybe Royal is at the heart of it, but I think I connect. And even if I don't, I can't feel okay with my brother being the target. No matter how much trouble he's gotten himself into."

"But if it doesn't have anything to do with you…"

She shook her head, her mouth wobbling just a second before she firmed it, straightened her shoulders, as if going to battle. "He's my brother, Zeke. What am I going to do? Just set it aside and ignore it? Pretend I'm not scared because he's a target and maybe I'm not? I can't. Could you?"

"No." He understood too well the reality of having your sibling in danger. He'd done a lot of things to keep Carlyle safe, and still he'd worried about her every step of the way. Hell, he still worried about her, even knowing she was in a good place over at the Hudson Ranch.

But Brooke worrying, being miserable, tied him into knots. He hated seeing her so damn sad. He reached out and rubbed a hand down her back, some pathetic attempt at comfort.

She didn't pull away. She even leaned into him a little bit.

And he just…had to help somehow.

"Let's see if Granger has a minute to talk. He helped you with Royal's lawyer, right? He's got some insight into Royal's charge and prison time. Maybe he can tug a line on something the cops can't. Make a connection we haven't seen. Granger and Shay are good at that."

Brooke hesitated. "I hate asking them to get reeled back into things they purposefully left behind."

Zeke laughed and gave her shoulders a squeeze before releasing her, because he needed his distance, or he'd want to… Well.

"They don't mind, Brooke. You know, Granger and Shay and a couple others jumped in to help my family when we finally found my mother's killer." Zeke thought about the gunshot wound he'd received for the trouble. About how close Carlyle and Mary had been to getting hurt. At how beat up Walker had felt after.

But they'd survived, because they'd worked together and because North Star had been there to help. Even after disbanding.

"We'd likely all have ended up dead if they hadn't helped. And I didn't have to beg. They were involving themselves before I even got half the request for help out of my mouth. It's hard to leave all this stuff behind, even when you want to. But even more than that, Brooke, we're all still a family."

"I had no problem leaving North Star danger behind," she said.

A bit stiffly, he noted, and with some of that old primness that might have made him smile if he didn't feel sorry for her. "Yes, the danger. I'm talking about the people, Brooke."

She expressly didn't meet his gaze. And maybe he shouldn't poke. She didn't need him to psychoanalyze her. She'd been *desperately* in love with him and he'd screwed it all up.

But she was here, and maybe he was old enough, mature enough, *finally*, to realize that life didn't present you with many opportunities for something good…so he probably shouldn't be afraid of them.

"And I know you stepped away from all the people

too." He'd kept in touch with everyone enough to know only Granger had been able to touch base with Brooke over the years. "But it wasn't because you wanted to."

"Oh, wasn't it?" she returned with that chin raised in that way she had. But she didn't meet his eyes because she knew he was right.

And he understood, in part, because he'd kept his own family at a certain kind of arm's length for a while there. Thinking if he hid who he was, what he felt, all that untenable *worry* that existed inside him, they'd be better off.

He'd learned the hard way, when they'd fought through a lot of danger to solve their mother's murder, he'd been wrong.

And Brooke was wrong to cut off people who cared about her. He understood why, but that didn't make her less wrong, and she should know it. Sometimes it took someone saying what you knew flat-out to you for you to finally accept it.

"You're always so afraid. That you might ask too much. That you have to walk on all those eggshells your foster families made you walk on. That if you're not perfect, people will turn you away. I suppose I didn't help that any. And I'm sorry. For a lot of things."

She looked at him now, blue eyes wide and startled. "I don't think now is the time to have some kind of postmortem about our relationship, Zeke."

"No, it isn't. But I'm going to take the opportunity anyway. Because it's here. I think you must know I didn't hurt you on purpose, or you wouldn't be here. You wouldn't have called me for help. Or maybe I just hope that. I had my own issues, which isn't an excuse. I'm still sorry."

She stood there, very still, but he knew she was absorbing what he'd said. Taking it in, sorting it through.

Her precious data points. And that was fine. He'd said what he'd needed to.

They could focus on the danger at hand now. So he led her to the living room and told her to take a seat on the couch while he grabbed his laptop. Once they settled together, hip to hip, with the computer on the coffee table, Zeke put in the video call to Granger. He was grateful the man answered right away.

Granger's expression registered some surprise, no doubt at seeing both of them on the screen, but then he just smiled. "Well, hello. It's nice to see you two together."

Neither Zeke nor Brooke said anything to that, but Zeke could see in the screen the bland kind of smile Brooke offered at those words. No point in arguing about *together*. But she didn't like it.

"Hey, Granger. We've got a…bit of a situation."

"Of course you do," he returned, mostly with humor. "Lay it on me."

Zeke relayed the information from the stalking to Royal to the car bomb. Brooke explained a little about what she was doing with the remains, and the skull.

She leaned forward, getting closer to the screen. "You helped me get Royal the lawyer, send those letters so they wouldn't be traced back to North Star at all. But he didn't get them, and he didn't know I was the source of the lawyer."

Granger frowned at that. "Not sure how that could have happened. I can go back and look into it. The lawyer. Where the letters would have gone through."

"And more into her father," Zeke added. Because if Royal thought this could involve old members of the Sons, why wouldn't they look into that? North Star might have destroyed a lot of their records, but Granger knew how to get any and all information on any old Sons's activity.

"He's still in jail," Brooke said tightly.

"Yeah, but if Royal thinks it might connect, we need to know... There's something with your family and their ties to the Sons going on here because of Royal. Let's find all the information we can, even if it ends up not connecting to the danger."

"Zeke's right," Granger said. "The more information, the better off you are. I'll see what Shay and I can come up with. We'll get back to you as soon as we can."

"You don't have to—"

"Brooke," Granger cut her off gently. "North Star might not exist anymore, but we're still a family. Always will be."

Zeke took Brooke's hand, squeezed it, tried to get that sentiment through to her. Regardless of...anything. They'd all been connected by something, and it didn't just go away because that something didn't exist anymore.

"We'll be in touch."

They said their goodbyes and Zeke closed the laptop. He looked at Brooke, hoping she'd seem more settled. Relieved or calm or something. Maybe she couldn't believe in all those things *he'd* said, but surely she believed in Granger.

If anything, she looked more upset.

"Brooke."

She jumped up and started pacing. "I just don't know what to do. I feel as powerless as when I was a kid." She made jerky movements with her hands as she moved back and forth, Viola following her path. "Everything is happening *to* me and I just—"

Zeke stood and stopped her by taking her hands in his. He gave them a reassuring squeeze. "Give yourself a break, Brooke. You've spent the past month studying a cave full of human remains. That's going to weigh on anyone."

"That's my *job*. And I'm good at my job," she said, looking up at him. Her eyes were filled with tears, but they didn't fall.

Maybe that killed him just as much as actual tears would have. He moved a hand over her hair. "Sweetheart." He remembered too late that she didn't want him to call her that anymore. But she didn't snap at him.

She leaned into him.

So he pulled her closer, wrapped his arms around her, hoping he could press some comfort into her. She didn't cry, she didn't speak. She just stood there with her cheek on his chest. And she breathed. In that old way of hers, careful in and out.

He could have stood with her in his arms for eternity. He'd been so afraid of that feeling four years ago. He didn't even know what had changed to make it not so terrifying right now. He still had no real future, no real plans. No way to fold her into his life.

But maybe he'd watched Walker and Carlyle find ways to belong to someone else and that had...opened something inside him.

It hardly mattered because Brooke was pulling away. He'd had his chance and he'd messed it up years ago. No going back and fixing that. He could protect her in the here and now, but he had to stop thinking about love and—

"Oh, to hell with it," she muttered, which sounded more like something he would have said.

But then her mouth was on his. Not wild and angry like the last kiss he'd initiated. Even when she *was* angry, that wasn't Brooke. This was soft, gentle. And, it turned out, everything he wanted. Softness and warmth. A sweetness he'd viewed as a weakness when they'd been together, even when he'd been attracted to it.

Yet here she was. Still so fully Brooke. Strong and smart and doing this incredible job, without hardening herself to anything.

It was a wonder. She was a wonder. And he wanted—

She pushed at his chest then stepped away from him when he released her. She took a few steps back. She inhaled shakily and looked at the front door as if expecting Hart and Royal to burst through at any minute. They wouldn't, but it also wasn't like this was some appropriate time to deal with…whatever was still between them.

Because it was *something*. But danger trumped it all.

"Do you have any ice cream?" she asked, chin up as if daring him to demand they talk this through.

The request made him laugh because he realized that any place he'd lived for any length of time, he'd kept ice cream on hand. Not for himself. He could take it or leave it. But ice cream had always been her favorite, her comfort food.

All these years and, somewhere hidden deep in his psyche, he'd been keeping ice cream in his freezer with her in mind. Wishing for this moment.

"Yeah. Let's have some ice cream."

Chapter Fourteen

Brooke worked very diligently not to think about the fact she'd kissed Zeke. She'd just set it aside. Pretended it hadn't happened.

Because this was like some kind of backsliding. Calling Granger for help. Falling all over again for this man. It was…a past she'd left behind. She couldn't fall back into it just because of some danger.

But it was a really good kiss.

And the fact of the matter was, she could keep pretending. She could convince herself Zeke hadn't thought of her in four years. She could try to tell herself this was just chemistry and it didn't matter.

But he had mint chocolate chip ice cream in his freezer.

She could convince herself she was being self-absorbed but knew Zeke had no great affinity for mint chocolate chip ice cream. It wasn't in there because of him.

That meant it was probably in there because of her. Like the eggs with cheese. Like all the details he seemed to remember so easily.

It's just food, Brooke. Get a grip. She didn't have the time or space to figure out Zeke. Or why the things he'd said about North Star and family and her fears felt like keys unlocking everything she'd kept hidden away for so long.

Or why him holding her felt like home. Kissing him felt like she'd just been on ice for four years, waiting around for this. For him. When she *hadn't* been.

She was relieved when Royal returned, no matter how angry he looked. He was here and she could stop thinking about Zeke and the past and focus on the important danger in their present.

"There was a tracker on my car," he said grimly. "Hart's sending it in to have it tested. See if they can get something out of it. He didn't seem too optimistic though."

Brooke didn't have the words for this development. She expected Zeke to say something, but he didn't. Not even to blame Royal for leading someone straight for her.

Nonetheless, that's what he'd done.

"It's late, guys," Zeke said. "Let's get some sleep. Reconvene in the morning with clear heads and maybe more information from Hart."

Brooke glanced at Zeke, but she couldn't quite read his expression. Except that it was *soft*. And he was being nice to Royal. And that almost made her cry.

"You can take the room next to Brooke's," he continued. "It's not in the best of shape, but there's a mattress in there. I'll rustle up some blankets and a pillow."

"Grab your bag. I'll show you where it is," she said to Royal. She didn't look at Zeke. Not even to thank him. She should have, but she was feeling too soft. And she had to find some way to be strong.

So, she led Royal upstairs, showed him the room next to hers. It indeed wasn't much, and she resisted the urge to offer to swap rooms. She didn't have to be a martyr to him just because of her guilt. When *he* should be feeling guilty, if anyone did.

Besides, Royal didn't complain. He dropped his bag.

He turned to her and studied her face as he crossed his arms over his chest. "Something going on between you two?"

It made her want to laugh, which was a surprising development in this whole confusing night. Like Royal was trying to play overprotective brother when they hadn't seen each other for so long, and never as adults. In her mind, he was still ten. Not this mountain of a tattooed man.

She supposed this was his way of caring, which made her response gentle. And the truth. Mostly.

"Not that it's any of your business, but no. There…was, a long time ago. But not anymore."

Royal made a considering noise, like he didn't buy it, and maybe he shouldn't since she and Zeke kept somehow falling into kissing each other. And she couldn't blame Zeke for that, because she'd initiated the last kiss.

A really, really brain-melting kiss that had only ended because she'd been afraid of where it might lead if she let it. Because it would be so easy to be in love with him again, to lean into all that.

She couldn't imagine surviving the heartbreak a second time. Maybe she was strong enough, but she was tired of the ways life seemed set up to break her. Her brother, case in point.

"Royal. Be upfront with me. What aren't you telling me?"

He paused for a moment, but he didn't look away. "Long story, Chick. And aren't we supposed to get some sleep?" He moved for the door, but she gave him a big-sister glare and he sighed.

"Those foster homes sucked," he said.

That was neither here nor there. But she'd let him start wherever he needed. "That they did."

He looked puzzled. "But you're like...some fancy scientist-type person."

Did he think that was because she'd had a *good* experience? "Getting an education didn't mean I was loved or taken care of, Royal. At a certain point, I was put in a position where failure was not an option." In some ways, she'd been grateful for the strictness of the final foster family she'd had in high school before she'd aged out. Their uncompromising and authoritarian methods had given her the ability to do something with her life. If she hadn't had that, who knows where she would have ended up.

But it had been a hard, cold, four years in that home. Where even the whiff of a B could have gotten her kicked back to a group home.

"I guess I never thought..." Royal trailed off, looking confused, but then he shook his head. "My point is, I hated them all. I never could fit in. I was always itching for a fight. So about the time I turned sixteen and I was back in one of those group homes, I figured I'd just run away and go back to the Sons. The system wasn't too broken up by my absence."

"Royal."

"I didn't go back to like belong or anything. I just thought about us. Growing up there. How bad it was, but how bad the foster shit was. So I figured... What if I went back? I could help kids like us. Be their inside protector. Without all the rules and school and constant interference by people who thought they were giving me charity. It was bad living with the Sons, sure, but not worse than being bounced around, knocked around. At least I had some...status there."

He'd chosen to go back because a system had failed him. It was hard to blame him for that, but... "You could have also chosen to go into law enforcement or social work and helped, Royal."

He snorted. "Yeah, right. *Rules* and me, Chick? We don't get along."

She resisted the urge to roll her eyes. Her brother was telling her what had happened to him, what he'd done. And she wanted to hear it. "So, you went back to Dad?"

"Yeah. I convinced Dad I really wanted back. Wanted to be a part of it. I didn't. I wanted to mess up his plans. I wanted to help kids like us. And the way they treated those girls…" He shook his head. "I just always saw you. So I had to do something. I spent a year doing that, always so afraid Dad saw right through me while I tried to protect those girls. I was always waiting for a real end, but in retrospect, I guess I fooled him."

A real end. Brooke looked at her brother, thought of Zeke. A death wish. The idea that if they died doing something noble, it would somehow make everything all right.

It made her want to cry for them. Maybe *all* of them.

But she could tell Royal all the things she couldn't tell Zeke. Because this was her baby brother and he'd done something noble, even if she wished he'd gone about it in a different way.

"I love you no matter what. I'd have gotten you that lawyer even if you'd been in the wrong. I don't know why it got kept from you that I was behind it, but it doesn't matter. What matters is, I was going to support you no matter what. I always will."

Royal sighed. "Because you think you owe me, Chick. And maybe I let you think that because it's easy, but you don't. We were both kids. Failed by a hell of a lot of people."

Brooke had to carefully inhale then force herself to

exhale at his words. She wanted it to be true, but... How could it be? She'd been older. She should have...fought harder. Done something. She didn't know how to explain that to him, and he was talking about the situation at hand anyway. Not their past.

"I don't think it matters how dismantled the Sons is. I disrespected Dad when I tricked him into letting me in then protected those kids. I embarrassed him in that circle. No amount of jail time is going to make him let that go, because it wasn't about the Sons. It was about him and me, and me pulling one over on him. Maybe he's still in jail right now. Maybe he has no ability to reach the outside, but I doubt it. I really doubt it. Men like that don't just stop being sadistic, Brooke."

It wasn't that she disagreed with him. She remembered just how vindictive their father could be. That's how he'd gotten Family Services called on him. How he'd managed to lose his kids no matter how the Sons had tried to wriggle him out of it. Because he'd been determined to make someone else *pay* for their lack of reverence. That had mattered more than any consequence to Jeremiah Campbell.

It was just that she hadn't known her brother as an adult. And he stood there looking and sounding like a *man*. It was disorienting.

"He's the only one who'd know you matter to me, Chick. Someone threatening you to me...it had to be him."

"Or come from him."

"Yeah. Look, leopards don't change their spots. Maybe the Sons is gone. Maybe he's in jail. But it doesn't mean he can't wield a certain group of people against us."

She didn't like it at all, but Royal was right. "Did you tell all this to Thomas?"

"Bits and pieces. Hart seems legit, for a cop, but…"

"I need you to tell him. Everything. Anything. No matter how little. We can't protect you if we don't know what this is. The police can look into Sons's things. They can look into all Dad's prison records. They can really dig into this and keep you safe in the process."

"What about you?"

"It's not about me. You said so yourself."

"No, I said our father is the only one who'd know that to hurt me he only had to get to you. That means *you're* in danger. I don't think he'd be too broken up about hurting you again, Brooke."

She didn't like the way her brother used her real name, though she couldn't pinpoint why. Only that it made this all so much more serious, when she didn't want him worried about *her*. She couldn't be a burden to him when…

Zeke's words from earlier came back to her.

You're always so afraid. That you might ask too much. That you have to walk on all those eggshells your foster families made you walk on. That if you're not perfect, people will turn you away.

Maybe she felt those things, but was it really wrong? Except she'd failed Royal before, and here he was and… It didn't matter. This wasn't about *her*. Even if she got caught in the crosshairs. "Okay, maybe, but—"

"You going to tell your boyfriend?"

She sighed. There was no point explaining, *again*, that Zeke was just…Zeke. Maybe the old feelings were still there, but… There was no ending that wasn't the exact same as four years ago.

Even if Zeke acted like he understood his mistakes. Even if he understood *her*. Even if he'd changed from that angry, edgy, desperate-to-*act* man.

Brooke was the same.

"Here's the deal," Royal said when she didn't answer. "I'll tell the cops everything, if you tell Zeke everything. No point leaving that guy out of it when it's clear he'll protect you."

"I've asked for his help in that department because he's perfectly capable, but—"

"He'd lick your boots, Chick. That's the only reason I'm under this roof, the only reason I haven't messed with him. He's only mixed up in this to save you from it. For whatever reason, that's your deal, but it's true."

That left her feeling too…something. Hopeful, probably. "We really do need to get some sleep."

He nodded. "That's fine. As long as we have a deal."

Brooke blew out a breath. Was there any point arguing? Maybe it was really best that everyone knew everything. "Fine."

"I'll talk to Hart tomorrow."

She nodded and then left him in the room, not sure what else to say. What else to do. Everything felt like such a jumble. One she couldn't list or organize or data point her way through like she had with studying the skull.

Still, she got ready for bed. Crawled into the nicer one than her brother's. She was exhausted and *needed* rest, but her mind whirled.

She thought about Zeke in his bedroom downstairs. Far away from Royal. Far away from the heavy things weighing her down.

He'd always been a safe place to land.

Except that whole time when he broke up with you and left you to pick up the pieces on your own.

But she wasn't that girl anymore, was she?

She could practically hear her old therapist's voice. *Be-*

ware self-destructive tendencies brought on by overstressing yourself to be perfect in everything and make everyone around you happy while ignoring your own happiness.

That's essentially what Zeke had accused her of as well. Because she did one of two things. Contorted herself for people or isolated herself from people.

She didn't think she'd done either with Zeke the past week. Wasn't that funny? And if she were to put her own happiness in the mix, wouldn't that include a late-night trip down to Zeke's bedroom? Because she was well versed in the ways that could make her happy.

Temporarily.

Like ice cream.

The ice cream he'd bought, thinking of her, whether he'd been conscious of it or not.

ZEKE TOSSED AND TURNED. Even though he'd been the one to suggest sleep, it felt too much like sitting around waiting for something to happen. Something to happen to *Brooke*.

He sat up, and the only reason he didn't reach for the gun on his nightstand was the little flash of something red he saw in the moonlight.

Brooke.

He pushed into a sitting position as she entered his room, and then she just stood there, a foot or two away from his bed.

Meanwhile his heart clattered against his chest like its own independent being.

"Everything okay?" he asked, his voice rusty.

"Yes," she said calmly. Firmly. "I was just talking to Royal when we went up, one-on-one, and we made a deal. He'd tell this all to Thomas, if I told it all to you."

Zeke wasn't sure what to expect "this all" to entail, but

he was more taken off guard by the fact Royal had suggested such a deal. "Why did he want you to tell me?"

"Well, he seems to think you'll protect me."

Zeke didn't think Royal had a particularly high opinion of him, so this was interesting. "He'd be right."

"I know. That *is* why I called you in the first place with this whole mess." She moved closer to his bed and then, to his great surprise, took a seat on the edge of it. Her hip touched his knee. Only a sheet between them.

He knew he couldn't sit there and ruminate on *that*, so he tried to focus on the facts. "So, what is this whole thing you have to tell me?"

She relayed Royal's involvement with the Sons before he'd gone to jail. Royal's relationship with their father and why their dad might make Royal, and thus Brooke, a target. It felt a bit like being back in North Star. Trying to untangle the petty infighting in the Sons. Make sense of where the real issues stemmed from.

And what the real consequences would be from angry men with more weapons than sense, and so much anger and bitterness it had stamped out any empathy they'd been born with.

It was never simple, and almost always involved the outsized egos of awful men.

"It won't be the Sons," Zeke said, trying not to be too aware of the fact he wore nothing but boxers and she was sitting on his bed in a dark room late at night. And it would only take peeling that sheet away for them to be touching.

The desperate, pounding need to touch her would have been distracting if he wasn't such a professional. Or so he told himself.

"They don't have that kind of reach anymore," he continued. "But there are other groups, other ways for a man to wield control from prison. I don't like it. Royal's right. You're *both* in danger and targets, until we figure out exactly where this threat is coming from."

"This isn't what you signed up for."

For a moment, he just stared at her shadow. Did she really not understand? "Brooke. You can't be serious. I signed up for *you.*"

She didn't say anything, and he couldn't see her expression in the dim room. When she didn't attempt to speak at all, he set out to reassure her. "You *and* Royal are safe here. We'll make sure of it."

She took one of her long, careful inhales. Let it out slowly. It reminded him too much of a time long gone, when she was just…in his life. In his bed. He'd wake up or fall asleep to her doing her deep breathing, so sure it "centered" her.

Still, she said nothing. Still, she sat on his bed.

Zeke waited for whatever else there was, but she just… never said anything else.

"This…couldn't have waited until morning?" He wasn't about to lie to himself. He was prodding.

"I suppose it could have. But I can't stop my brain from whirling in the same ridiculous circles, and I just couldn't lay there anymore marinating in my own…unsolvable problems. So, I figured I'd tell you."

"Ah." He waited. She didn't leave. Didn't offer anything else. "Well, you've told me."

"Yes," she agreed. And didn't so much as shift a muscle as if considering getting up.

He had a few options. The smart one would be to maintain *his* silence. Wait for her to say whatever she wanted to say, do whatever she wanted to do.

Had he ever been able to maintain *smart* when it came to her? No. Because even when he'd made what had felt like the right decision at the time to put distance between them years ago, he'd handled it badly. He'd hurt her *badly*.

If he was smart, if he was strong, if he was actually any of the things he prided himself on being, he'd have the control to keep his mouth shut.

But he was nothing he thought he was or wanted to be when it came to her. "Are you trying to tell me you came down here looking for a distraction?"

She made a little noise. Not quite a laugh, but close. "Maybe." She shifted. She touched his chest and flattened her palm over his heart. "Yes, that is what I'm saying. Going to kick me out?"

He circled his fingers around her wrist, pulled her into him. Over him. "I'd be your distraction a million times over, Brooke. No questions asked."

And he spent the night keeping that promise.

Chapter Fifteen

Zeke woke up while it was still dark out, with an empty side of the bed. For a moment, he just stared. The room was dim, but he could make out the rumpled sheets, the indentation in the pillow on that side. A faint floral scent lingering in the air.

He hadn't dreamed it. Probably.

But where had she gone?

He got up, pulled on some clothes, and went in search of her. Not because he needed her to have some sort of postmortem, discuss what this was, what this meant. Just because he had to know she was okay.

At least, that's what he convinced himself of as he moved through the living room, the kitchen. He was about to get really desperate and creep upstairs to see if she'd gone to sleep in her own bed, but he noticed the front door was unlocked.

He'd checked all the locks at least three times last night before she'd come down to his room.

Surely that meant she'd left the house on her own accord. Maybe she'd gone to the barn to work in her lab. But her purse was right there and a quick look through it told him her key to the barn door was still in it.

So, she'd left for some other reason. But *why*? If she'd bolted because…

Well, he'd find her. He didn't care what it took. Maybe she didn't want it or like it, but he was hardly going to let her...

He pushed out the front door and then came to an abrupt halt.

She sat on the rickety porch, in the rocking chair that Carlyle had put there a month back, telling him he'd needed it because he was an old man now. Viola lay at her feet.

Brooke was watching the hint of a sunrise in the east. Or had been, until she'd looked over at him when he'd stormed out.

She raised an eyebrow, clearly at the way he'd burst out the door. "Everything okay?"

"Yeah... I just..." He didn't have the words. Her hair was tangled. She was wearing his hoodie—way too big for her small frame. She had her legs curled up under her and the sunrise seemed to burnish her gold. Ethereal.

He didn't have words for the emotion that swamped him. The *need* clogged in his throat. How much he wanted this. All those things he'd told her he'd never be able to give her four years ago.

And now he couldn't think of a single thing he wanted more.

She sighed heavily. Her gaze moved back to the sunrise, but her words were careful. Deliberate.

"I know what this is, Zeke. I know what last night was. It doesn't have to be all dramatic this go-around. I'm under no...illusions this is going to be something more than what it is."

"Which is?" he returned, not comfortable with the dispassionate way she'd delivered all that.

"A momentary...trip down memory lane." She said it

with one of her patented nods, like she could make things true through sheer force of will. "It was a great…interlude. No guilt. No drama. Just…a distraction. Like you said."

"That's *not* what I said."

Her head whipped back to look at him. Clearly an argument was on the tip of her tongue. He didn't let her mount it.

"I asked if that's what you were suggesting. And that's fine. If that's all you want it to be. I can deal." Maybe he'd find some way to deal. Because he supposed he deserved that.

But Zeke Daniels didn't go down without a fight. Why let that change?

"A distraction is not what I'm after though." He didn't know how to do this. How had Walker and Carlyle just… said the things that needed saying to deal with the people they loved? How had they made it all work?

Oh God, was he going to have to ask them?

"What *are* you after, Zeke?" she asked, sounding tired. "Another few months where we're in each other's pockets, pretending to have this…relationship, this domestic thing we never got as kids? Until the danger is gone and reality seeps in and now you don't even have North Star to blame for not being able to have a future. So then what?"

He deserved every single thing she was saying, even if every single word hurt. It's exactly what he'd done back then. But this wasn't back then. "Do you really think I haven't changed?"

She inhaled sharply, though her words remained very, very calm. "Maybe you have, but…" She looked so pained, so confused, so lost. And he had felt all those things. Every moment since the last time he'd seen her. He had convinced himself it didn't matter. It would never matter. He was such a lone wolf.

Yet what had he done? Settled down in the same place as his siblings with some vague idea to start a life. With some…nebulous hope something like Brooke would come along again.

Or maybe, deep down, he'd always just hoped for her.

But on the other side of all that was *her*. What she'd done in their time apart. What she'd thought. And the fact he'd had her trust once and broken it. She shouldn't so easily believe him this go-around. He knew that.

He also knew what it was like to hurt her, and he didn't want to live with that again. That pain had been worse than his fear, his inability to deal with everything he'd felt for her.

And, he supposed, that pain had brought him here. So he tried to find the words to get it across. To make her understand.

"I bought a ranch, Brooke. I put down roots. I sure as hell don't know what to do with them, but they're there."

"Okay," she said, nodding, though he knew her easy agreement wasn't going to go in his favor. She met his gaze with dark blue eyes. Sad, sad eyes. "But they're not *my* roots."

He should leave it at that. He *should*. But he couldn't.

"They could be."

BROOKE DIDN'T KNOW what she was doing. She didn't know what *they* were doing. Why either of them thought now was the time or that this conversation was a good idea. It would only make working together uncomfortable.

And she couldn't blame him because *she* had gone to

his room last night. She'd done that, and on purpose. She had gotten the exact result she'd wanted last night.

She'd woken up…with none of the expected regrets she thought she should feel. It had been too…wonderful to be back in his arms, back in his bed. Relive all the things they could give each other.

It hadn't been a distraction. It had been like coming home. Roots.

They could be yours.

But, without regret, she had to focus on reality. On keeping her feet and expectations grounded. They'd been down this road before. He'd ridden out the chemistry, and she'd let herself believe it was love.

She couldn't make the same stupid mistake again.

Even if he was standing there saying all the right things. All the right things she wished he'd said four years ago.

She hadn't expected this. She didn't know how to weather it. Not with everything else going on.

She pushed herself out of the chair. "I have to get ready. I want to get an early start at the cave. Detective Delaney-Carson is picking me up soon."

He didn't argue with her, didn't push the point of their relationship…whatever it was. He nodded, his dark eyes never leaving her face. "I could drive you down to the cave."

"I know, but I'm going to ask you for an even bigger favor."

He studied her like he couldn't possibly think of one, so he didn't fully believe her. But it was a huge favor for her, and it required trusting him the only way she knew how.

To protect someone she loved.

"Watch Royal for me. I just need to know there's someone here who'll stop him from flying off the handle, given the chance. I think… I think he wants to do the right thing, but I wouldn't put it past him to do the wrong one, thinking it was right."

"I guess I know a little about that."

Her mouth curved in spite of the riot of feelings inside her. Zeke did indeed.

Could she really believe he'd changed? She knew he was different. There was a…stillness to him he hadn't had four years ago. Still tense, still serious, still *very* protective. But not quite so…pumping with unleashed energy. Not so desperate to *act*.

Did that equal change? She wasn't sure she could come to a conclusion on that and believe in it. It required her to be…certain and sure. With everything else going on? How could she be sure of *anything*?

"I'll keep an eye on him," Zeke promised. "And look, we can pretend last night didn't happen. We can do whatever you want, Brooke, and I mean that. Because I care about you. I never stopped thinking about you. I made a mistake, a lot of mistakes."

She didn't know what to say. Maybe nothing. Especially when he kept talking.

"I don't make the same mistakes twice."

He said it like a promise, like a vow. And she wanted to be stronger than the woman who fell for that line, but look at him. All serious. All…perfect. He'd always been just what she wanted.

Remember how hard it was to get over that?

The Zeke of old had never made a promise that didn't have to do with her physical safety. He was right the other day when he'd told her he'd never said he hadn't loved her back then, because he'd never used the word *love*.

And he still wasn't saying it. He was saying a lot of sweet, important things. But not the main one.

"I don't know what I want, Zeke. Except to solve this case. To figure out who's after me or Royal or whatever this is. Maybe after that…I can figure out what we are."

He nodded, his hands shoved deep in his pockets.

She'd expected an argument. Or did she want one? Because an argument would solidify her feelings, but him agreeing with her just left her even more confused.

But she had *work.* Important work. She marched herself inside and got dressed for the day. She grabbed her laptop and took it out to the barn, avoiding everyone. Even the dog.

Holed up in the makeshift lab, Brooke opened the report the lab in Cheyenne had sent her this morning. She read through the report, took notes, lost herself in the work. Putting the data points together.

There was no way some of the bones in the cave didn't precede Jen Rogers. It wasn't Brooke's job to come up with a second suspect. It was just her job to compile and analyze the data.

She put together as much of her own report as she could—this one geared to the detectives with enough laymen's terms they wouldn't be lost by the science. Anything admitted to court would need to be more scientific, but they needed another suspect before they could worry about *court.*

Luckily, Jen Rogers had confessed to the Hudson murders, so there was no way a second suspect got her out of trouble. This just…compounded the trouble.

A knock sounded at the barn door and, a second later, Zeke stuck his head in. "Detective's here to pick you up."

"Oh. Right. I'll be out in just a second." She glanced

at where she was storing the skull. She still hadn't confessed to the detectives she'd taken it, run her own tests.

Now wasn't the time for that anyway. That was for another day. Today was for more excavating. It was for focusing on *one* problem, not the cascade of others.

She greeted Detective Laurel Delaney-Carson with a smile. She'd worked with Thomas more than Laurel the past few weeks, but she'd been more with Laurel the first few, so they were on friendly, comfortable terms.

They chatted about the weather and trivial things before easing into the case.

"I've got a little update on the scrapbook," Laurel offered as she drove. "Dahlia is still doing some digging into the facts behind who the two men were in the picture that might be in the cave, if the label is right and all that, but it looks like the picture was taken in the thirties. Maybe early forties," she said.

Brooke considered the picture. There wasn't a good way to judge the age of the men, at least to Brooke's eye, and no doubt Dahlia would find more information as she researched, but Brooke didn't think those men in the photograph could have been any younger than twenty. That meant, even if that picture was dated into the forties, the youngest either of those men could be now was well over a hundred.

And her preliminary examination of the skull lent itself to her believing it had been *buried* closer to a hundred years ago. That meant...

"If the bones are as old as the picture, we might be looking at a suspect who's long dead." Or worse, a series of murderers who used the same place as their dumping grounds. Purposefully, maybe.

"And spent their life getting away with murder?" Laurel scowled as they drove into the nature preserve. "I don't like that."

"Has anyone questioned Jen Rogers about the scrapbook?"

"We've tried. Last month when she was first arrested, we tried to get her to explain why she would steal it from us. Obviously, she wasn't too keen on letting us in. Unfortunately, with her murder case so open and shut, there's no real leverage on our end to get her to explain now."

Brooke considered keeping her theory to herself. She'd fought so hard in her position, and it required a lot of evidence and not a lot of *theory* on her part. She'd worked with several detectives who'd only wanted the facts. Not her *take*.

But Thomas and Laurel hadn't been like that, and maybe everything the past few days was trying to teach her to stop being so damn self-reliant. To let people in. To *trust*.

She thought of Zeke saying he didn't make the same mistake twice. The way he'd held her when she'd cried. Last night in his bed and...

Good *lord*, now was not the time to be thinking about her personal life. She tried to organize her thoughts on the *case*, but Laurel pulled up to the cave entrance where usually a pair of deputies were stationed.

Not today.

"I don't like that," Laurel said, a frown on her face as she slowed the cruiser to a stop. "Nothing came over the radio about them leaving their post."

She picked up the radio in her car. Brooke didn't follow all the little codes she used, but she got the gist that Laurel was trying to figure out where the deputies had gone and asking a few more to come out. Brooke didn't think the assigned officers were responding.

"We're going to stay right here until we know what's going on," Laurel said. She sounded and appeared calm, but it didn't escape Brooke's notice that her hand now rested on the butt of her weapon as her gaze scanned the world outside her cruiser.

So Brooke looked out into the sunny day as well. Was there another threat out there? Would she ever really be free of them?

Chapter Sixteen

Zeke didn't like feeling like a babysitter, but he'd made a promise to Brooke, so he stuck close to the house and made sure to keep an eye on any and all exits so he would know if Royal tried to bolt. So far, Royal hadn't even ventured outside the house. Zeke wasn't even sure he'd left his room.

With the noonday sun hanging over the ranch, a car pulled up the gravel drive. Zeke had hoped for an early return from Brooke, but it wasn't her. It was Carlyle.

She came to a stop close to the house, hopped out. "Brought more dog food."

He was about to give her a hard time for showing up unannounced, but... Well, maybe they weren't the talk-through-our-problems type of family, but they *could* be. He'd told Brooke he'd changed, so maybe he needed to change in all things. Maybe his sister, who was *engaged*, could offer some...advice.

Little as he liked admitting to her he needed some. But if it was for Brooke, wouldn't he suffer any embarrassment or discomfort?

"Thanks, Car. Hey, listen—"

They both looked over at the front door as it squeaked open. Royal stood there, making no bones about checking Carlyle out.

"Something Brooke should know about?" Royal called out across the yard.

Zeke supposed there was no reason to be irritated. He should be glad Royal would feel protective at all over Brooke. "I'm pretty sure she's aware my sister comes by from time to time."

"Sister," Royal said, nodding slightly. Then he flashed a grin right at Carlyle. "Hey. Luckily you don't look a *thing* like your brother."

She rolled her eyes. "I don't know who you are, but I don't like you."

"*Brooke's* brother," Zeke supplied.

"Oh." She grimaced. "Maybe I'll reserve judgment. But don't grin at me like that or you'll meet the snapping jaws of my fiancé's rabid dog pack."

Royal rocked back on his heels. He didn't stop grinning, but he gave Carlyle a little salute. "Message received."

"I should hope so," she muttered. She turned to her truck, lowering the gate so Zeke could grab the bag of dog food out of the bed. He hefted it up and over his shoulder.

"You want some breakfast?" he asked his sister.

She eyed him suspiciously. "Already ate. What's up with you?"

"Nothing's *up* with me."

"You've literally spent every second I'm here trying to get rid of me since the day you bought the place, and now you're inviting me for breakfast. Something is up."

He shrugged. "Just wanted to talk."

"Yes, also your favorite thing to do. Us talking is such a common occurrence. How silly of me to be suspicious." She rolled her eyes again.

He scowled at his sister. "Are you going to take this once-in-a-lifetime opportunity to give me advice or what?"

She looked at him then the house. Royal had disappeared back inside, but Viola was racing around the yard excitedly now. "We going to do this while you're hefting a fifty-pound bag of dog food?"

"Walk with me then." She fell into step beside him as he walked toward the house. "You ever screw things up with Cash?" he asked, hoping she wouldn't horrify him with details and make him regret this whole thing.

"Nah, I'm perfect."

Zeke didn't bother to sigh. "He ever screw things up with you?"

"Let me guess. This heart-to-heart has something to do with your little redhead?"

"You're *so* astute." He dropped the bag of dog food inside the back door of the screened-in porch. Then he kept walking, because all this was *his*. Those roots he'd told Brooke he'd made, even if he didn't know what to do with them.

And he still didn't, except that he wanted her here. Tangled in them. With him.

"Look, love's a mess. So you'll screw it up all the time." Carlyle made a kind of *what can you do* hand gesture. "The trick is just figuring out how, and not being afraid to admit that you might be the problem."

"I know I'm the problem," he grumbled, shoving his hands into his pockets.

"You? With your winning personality and ability to verbalize emotion and empathy so well? This is a shock."

"You going to give me a break?"

She grinned at him, humor dancing in her eyes. "Nah."

"Cool. Maybe I'll talk to Walker."

That earned him an even bigger eye roll. "We're not like Walker."

"We're not?"

"No. Walker is a…what would you call it? Caretaker. He's mush on the inside. Always has been, no matter how tough he tried to be on the outside."

That was fair and true. Zeke had always considered Walker the best of them, personality-wise. Not perfect or anything, just…more whole, he supposed. He didn't know why he was surprised to hear Carlyle say the same. "And what are we?"

"Less mush. More razor blade. Can't expose that vulnerable underbelly, right?"

Zeke shrugged even though he supposed that was the crux of it all. Those soft feelings he'd spent his whole life hiding—with razor blades, he reckoned—to protect himself from everything out there.

"And that's what you gotta do with love. Show the vulnerabilities. There's no getting around it. Sucks, but that's life."

"I already sort of messed things up with her once. A while back."

"Ah," she said, as if that explained everything. "So, it's not just current you that's the problem. It's past you. And past you was kind of a dick."

He scowled at her, but she shrugged. "Hey, the *kind of* was me trying to be nice."

Zeke didn't bother to respond to that. It wasn't *untrue*, though he wasn't sure it was *fair* of feral Carlyle to call him out on it.

"Not much experience in the mending-a-broken-heart thing," she continued. "But I guess it's the same as anything else, except with more patience. You love someone, you be there for them, and you tell them. You can't make them get it through their thick skulls. That's gotta be on them."

Tell them. Zeke grimaced. He'd always felt like *love* was a kind of bad word. The sort of thing that had messed his mother up so much she'd gotten herself mixed up with two useless criminals—who'd worked together to end her life.

Zeke *loved* Brooke, because he didn't have another word for the feeling, but saying it felt like…well, he guessed what Carlyle had said. Exposing a soft, vulnerable underbelly when he'd spent his life putting armor around it.

"It's not a magic word, I guess. But if it's real, if you mean it, it feels pretty damn close. And it can heal a lot of broken things. Not all of them, but a lot of them."

They'd come full circle around the house and back to her truck, and she'd been very real, very honest, very her. Somewhere along the instability, fear and danger of their childhood, she'd turned into this stable, adjusted *woman*. He'd always known Walker had that kind of thing in him, but to see Carlyle step into her own, and still be herself, was a confidence boost.

He reached out, took her left hand and jiggled the finger that had a ring on it. An *engagement* ring. So incongruous to everything he thought they'd have. "You really going to do the whole *Mrs.* thing?"

"Don't forget stepmom thing. We'll have a high schooler next year."

When in so many ways Carlyle was still a teenager to him, even if she was in her midtwenties now. But here she was saying things like *We'll have.*

"Izzy's a good kid," he offered, because he liked Cash's daughter. And more, he knew Carlyle loved the girl.

"The best," Carlyle replied brightly.

"And I guess Cash is all right."

She grinned at him. "Didn't need the stamp of approval, but I like it anyway." She moved forward then, after a pause, wrapped him in a hug. "You're a good guy, Zeke. Don't forget it. And don't be afraid to grovel." She pulled back, slapped his arm. "I like what little I've seen of her."

She opened her truck door. This grown woman with a settled, full life that made her happy. And she'd done that mostly on her own.

"Proud of you, Car."

She hesitated only a moment before she climbed the rest of the way into her driver's seat. "Then make me proud of you, Zeke," she returned before closing the door and driving away.

Zeke blew out a breath. Now he just had to figure out *how*.

Love.

Hell of a thing.

THE TWO DEPUTIES who'd originally been assigned to guard the crime scene had returned, and Laurel was talking with them. She didn't look happy, but Brooke just sat in the car pretending to work on her laptop.

What she was really doing was watching the interaction. The deputies looked chagrined. Laurel was *pissed*.

Brooke studied their surroundings from her seat. The preserve was so big, the cave a vast system below it. It gave her a shiver to think about, to remember the day she'd come out of the cave feeling like she was being watched.

But that had likely just been Royal. There was no one

out there. There was no threat to her...well, that had to do with her work anyway.

Laurel stalked back to the cruiser and got into the driver's seat rather than gesture for Brooke to get out.

"They claim it was only a few minutes. One of them had to use the restroom, the other heard something and went to check it out. But I don't like the idea of you going in there when the entrance was left unguarded, even if it was brief. If we're dealing with a second suspect..." Laurel hesitated, shaking her head. "There's just no way to make a clean sweep of the cave and make sure no one went in. It's too big. The other entrances and exits are far away, and you'd have a hell of a time making it from one to another, but... It's too risky."

Brooke nodded. But, man, she wanted to get some work done today. "I'd like to point out that this second suspect was killing before Jen Rogers, Laurel. I don't have the data to back this up, so everything I'm saying is supposition, but if those pictures in the scrapbook connect, we really are talking about a suspect who would have to be dead by now."

Laurel took a few minutes, clearly thinking it over. "Jen Rogers lived in that cave for years. Undetected. Who knows what pieces we're still missing. That cave system is huge. I don't like unnecessary risks, Brooke."

"But if the cave system is too big that we can never be fully sure it's clear of people, how will I ever finish my work?"

Laurel scowled even deeper. "I know you're right, but I don't like this." She tapped her fingers on the steering wheel. "Okay, we'll go in. But we'll bring in more deputies. At least three plus me."

"That's a lot of manpower."

"This is our biggest case right now. Well-justified man-power. We can borrow from Sunrise and Hardy if we need to."

Brooke waited patiently while Laurel got more men situated. They did a sweep of the cave as best they could, and then finally Brooke was allowed to go in and set up. By the time she was ready enough to get to work, it was nearing lunchtime.

She could be annoyed about that later. Right now, she had to get to work. Not for the skull this time, but for the square she'd designated. Maybe she wanted to search for a body that would match the skull, but that wasn't how the job worked. She had to follow the standards set out by her profession, by her studies. If she looked for some-thing specific, she might miss something just as, if not more, important.

So, she got to work in the meticulous fashion she'd learned, carefully moving through sediment, on the look-out for more remains.

After a while, as she moved from one section to an-other, Brooke caught a glint of something out of the corner of her eye. She turned toward it. In the same exact spot the scrapbook had been wedged, there was a tiny silver item. Brooke leaned closer to inspect it. A…thimble? But not a working thimble. No, like a piece from…a board game.

She reached out then thought better of it. Because someone had put it there purposefully. Just like the scrap-book, but only *since* the scrapbook. Because she would have seen this before today if it had been there before.

Someone had been in and out of these caves just as much as she had been.

Or maybe someone had been in and just never out. Laurel had said Jen Rogers had lived in here for *years*.

Maybe the police had done their best to search for anyone else, but no one could guarantee there was no one
else here. Deep inside.

Brooke sucked in a breath. "Laurel? Can you come
over here?"

The detective was quick to move to her side. Brooke
pointed to the game piece. "This is exactly where I found
the scrapbook. And it was not here then or since."

Laurel's expression was grim. She didn't say anything
but photographed the area before pulling on gloves and
picking up the item and putting it in an evidence bag.

"Can we get tests run on it right now?" Brooke asked.

"It's so small. I'm not sure we'll get a print off of it.
Brooke, I don't like this. I think we should get out of here."

It felt like such a waste. To just get started and then to
pack everything up again, but this was concerning. So, she
agreed. "I have to pack up though. Especially if someone
is in and out, I want to make sure I'm not leaving anything
behind. And we're photographing everything."

They all got to work, the other deputies helping Brooke
by carting out the packed-up tools while Laurel photographed everything.

"Do you think someone is trying to send some kind
of…message?" Brooke asked as she turned off one of her
lights, folded it up and handed it to a deputy.

"With board games?" Laurel returned.

"I don't know. But someone put that scrapbook there—
and it couldn't have been there that long before I found it
or there'd be more damage to it. The thimble is new since
two days ago."

"Maybe it's just a sign that someone else is in here. You
grab that light and I'll grab this one and we'll be done."

They didn't turn off the lights or dismantle them, just

carried them toward the narrow pathway that led back outside.

Brooke heard a strange rumble and then the clatter of pebbles falling, scattering. It almost sounded like some kind of earthquake, but the ground didn't move even as rocks fell from above. "That's...not good."

"No. It's—" But she didn't finish her sentence. Instead, Laurel shoved her back, hard. It didn't take long for Brooke to figure out why, even as she stumbled onto her butt and let out a yelp of pain.

A big boulder fell right at her feet. More rocks were falling, pelting her in the head. It was some kind of... cave-in.

There had been a survey of the safety of the cave before she'd been cleared to excavate. Every report had determined it was stable and perfectly safe to work in.

Were they wrong, or had something...caused this?

Well, it didn't really matter, did it? The rocks were piling up. Laurel was shouting directions at her deputies, but Brooke was afraid to follow as huge pieces of rock rained down between her and Laurel.

She scooted farther back into the cave. Maybe it was the wrong move, but the rocks stopped pelting her here. Her head throbbed from where one had really gotten her good.

But she couldn't go deeper into the cave. She had to get *out*. She reached up, touched the throbbing spot on her head. Her hand came away sticky. That wasn't good.

Brooke pushed to her feet, grabbing the light she'd lost a grip on. She shone it in front of her.

A wall of rocks. There were a few spots at the top that were maybe holes she could get to or through, but she'd have to climb up something to reach them. She'd have to try to move the rocks, but would that cause more of a cave-in?

Panic was crawling up her throat, but not at being caved-in. No. This was worse.

So much worse.

There were sounds coming from behind her. Like footsteps. Splashing in the pools of water. *Squelch, tap. Squelch, tap.*

Fear seized her, but she forced herself to look over her shoulder.

A small, bent-over man was making his way toward her—illuminated by an actual torch he carried as well as the light of hers that still functioned.

"Well, hello." His smile showed off rotted teeth, his beard was long and matted. His eyes were wild, even if he spoke in a calm, singsongy voice. "Welcome to my home."

Chapter Seventeen

"What are we going to do? Just sit around and talk about the damn Sons all day?" Royal demanded irritably while Zeke sat calmly—if he did say so himself—at a table trying to compile Royal's information on his old gang involvement. On who, besides their father, might see Brooke as a viable way to hurt Royal.

"What would you rather do?" Zeke replied. "Let Brooke continue to be a target because of you?"

Royal scowled and crossed his arms over his chest. But he didn't mount another argument or complaint. Though he did mount an accusation. "You sure know a lot about how the Sons works."

"North Star ring any bells?"

Royal frowned then studied Zeke with some renewed interest. "That group that took them down. Vigilante stuff."

Zeke shrugged. "I wouldn't call it that. I'd call it a group of people with military and law-enforcement training who didn't have to get caught up in government red tape in order to launch a campaign to eradicate a threat to the safety of thousands of citizens."

Royal rolled his eyes. "Yeah, there's a real difference. You're telling me you were part of that?"

"Till the day they disbanded. Long *after* they eradicated the Sons."

Royal shook his head. "You don't understand. There's no *eradicating* cockroaches."

"Maybe not, but there's certainly cutting off all their sources of power so all they are is little annoying pests running around. Easily squashed by any errant boot."

Royal didn't have an argument for that and before Zeke could press again for more details about their father's role in the Sons, they both turned toward the telltale rumble of tires on gravel.

Zeke looked out the window to see Carlyle's truck. He wasn't sure why she'd returned so soon, but maybe she'd forgotten something. "Be right back."

He got up and went outside.

Royal followed him. "Your sister's hot," he offered as Carlyle hopped out of the truck.

"I don't even have to threaten you to shut your mouth, because even if her fiancé could take you, even if our older brother would beat him to it, Carlyle would take you out in a heartbeat." But any humor Zeke had for the situation died at the look on Carlyle's face as she jogged over to them.

"There was some kind of cave-in while Brooke was working," she said with no preamble. "Chloe got a call to come in for backup. I'm obviously not supposed to tell you that, but I was there when it happened and I thought you would want to know."

Zeke was halfway to his truck before she'd even finished speaking. *Cave-in?* What the hell did that mean? How could that happen? More importantly, how could he help?

"I'm coming with," Royal said, leveraging himself into the passenger side of the truck just as Zeke climbed into the driver's seat.

"Me too," Carlyle said.

Zeke opened his mouth to argue with his sister then shook his head. What was one more person? Particularly someone sneaky and on his side. Because he knew as well as anyone that he, Royal and Carlyle had no business being down at that cave.

But they were damn well going to be.

He began driving for the preserve, the word *cave-in* rattling around in his mind. "Anyone else stuck in there with her? The detective or the deputies?"

"I don't have all the details. Chloe didn't want to tell me. Probably for this reason right here," Carlyle said, gesturing at the three of them hurtling down the highway.

It curdled in his gut like acid that Brooke might be alone. That she might be hurt.

Or worse.

He refused to take that thought onboard. He'd tear every rock out of the way with his bare hands if he had to.

"I'm sure the park rangers or naturalists know what to do. They're like cave experts or whatever," Carlyle offered, though Zeke knew her well enough to know she was saying this for his benefit and not that she trusted anyone to be an expert on anything. "I'm sure they've dealt with cave-ins before. They must be a natural occurrence."

"We don't know that it *was* a natural occurrence," Zeke returned, keeping his grip tight on the steering wheel as he sped down the highway. "She's investigating mass murder. She's been a target thanks to her brother over here."

Carlyle didn't have anything to say to that, and if Royal had a reaction, Zeke was too focused on the road to notice it.

"Remember when we were looking for Jack and Chloe?" Carlyle said, leaning between the front seats. She pointed at the road ahead. Last month he and Carlyle had helped the Hudsons search for their missing brother.

"Yeah, I remember."

"They found Hart on the west side by the highway, right? After that woman knocked him out and dumped him. I remember there was a little access road for state employees on the map we looked at. I think it's coming up on the left."

Zeke nodded and, once he saw it, took the turn probably a little too hard. There was a No Trespassing sign posted, and a half-gate that was easy enough to off-road around.

"We have to be careful about how we approach, or we're going to get kicked out," Carlyle warned him. "They'll be set up at the cave entrance. We can't go there directly. At least, not all of us. They won't let us help. That, I know."

"I'd like to see them try to kick me out," Royal grumbled darkly.

"Noble and all, but they'll be wasting precious time and resources focused on you when we want them all focused on Brooke," Carlyle said, doing a much better job than Zeke was of staying calm. "There's a map at that trailhead we were at, do you remember?" she asked Zeke. "It had the whole cave system mapped out. With different entrances."

"I also recall the warning that trying to make your way through the cave system has resulted in death." But he followed the service road to the main road and, instead of heading straight to the cave entrance, took a turn that would lead them to the trailhead Carlyle was referencing.

He parked the truck, but left it running, and they all got out to look at the big board with the cave system map. They peered at it.

"Four natural entrances, and that's just what they put on the map," Royal said. "I did some exploring on the west one, to see if I could meet up with her inside and out of sight, but I didn't get very far."

"Scared of the dark?" Carlyle asked with a smirk.

"No doubt they've got cops at all these entrances now," Zeke said, ignoring them both. He'd poked around the east entrance when he'd been watching Brooke. Funny—or not—how he and Royal had essentially been following her in the same way.

Zeke studied the map. The south entrance was a possibility. It would take considerable time and skill to make it from the back of the cave to the front of the cave where Brooke was situated, so why would the rescue start there when there were closer places to get to her from?

"We're going to try this one." He pointed to the map. Right under the dire warning about exploring the cave on your own without any equipment. How dangerous it was. How easy to get lost.

"Let's go," Royal said.

He glanced at Carlyle, who shrugged. "Some backup wouldn't hurt, but I'm all for it."

"Text Walker. He can round up whatever Hudsons won't cause a fuss." Zeke pulled out his own phone. He didn't have much service, but hopefully enough to get a message off to Granger.

You know of anyone in the area? Brooke needs help at the cave.

He didn't bother to send any other details. Granger knew where they were and where Brooke was working. If he knew any former operatives—from his North Star days, or DEA days, or whatever and however Granger knew and collected people—who weren't too far away, he'd send them to help.

"All right," Zeke said, shoving his phone back in his pocket. "Sooner we get started, the better."

Carlyle patted her hip. "I'm armed. What about you two?"

Royal hesitated then lifted his shirt to reveal a holster with a gun in it. Zeke sighed, walked back to the truck, unlocked his glove compartment and got his gun out.

"Let's go."

BROOKE PRESSED HER back to the rocks that had trapped her inside. Some of the smaller ones gave a little and cascaded down to her feet, but most held firm. A wall she couldn't scale to get out of here.

The old man stood all the way across this particular "room" in the cave. There was a narrow hallway behind him that she'd planned to explore once she'd completely excavated this "room."

Maybe she was glad now that she hadn't. Because she did not think this man had happened upon one of the other natural, inhospitable entrances and all the signage warning against going too deep in the cave system.

No, he didn't look like he'd seen the outside of this cave in a long time. And that gave her the feeling that he might have had something to do with the sheer amount of bones buried inside.

"You've been doing a lot of digging in my front yard, young lady. I can't say as I appreciate it. I've worked very hard to landscape." Then he cackled like he'd told a joke.

"Do you live down here?" she asked, trying to sound calm.

"I don't just *live* down here, I *thrive* down here." He

spread his arms wide. "Do you know how many people wander into these caves—purposefully and not—and make themselves easy pickings to the god of the cave?"

Brooke had been part of North Star. She had training. She knew how to deal with a threat. She knew how to protect herself. She would not let herself panic. She would engage with this man while her brain whirled for a way out. "The god of the cave?"

He smiled again. "Me."

Okay, so she was dealing with…actual psychosis. She wasn't sure if that was better or worse than a murderer with a sound mind. If he really thought he was the god of the cave, how could she predict anything he did?

She had to fall back on that North Star training. She'd mainly been in the lab. A scientist, not an operative, but she'd still had to be trained on how to deal with danger. And she'd lived in Zeke's pocket while he'd been protecting her.

Granted, from a with-it criminal who'd just wanted to silence her or to stop her from finding the evidence the case needed. Not someone who was just…unhinged. And perhaps a serial killer.

That meant it was probably in her best interest to remain calm, to play along. "What should I call you?" She half expected him to give her some ridiculous godlike name, but the one he gave her was a shock.

"Leon Rogers."

Rogers, like Jen, clearly, but also like that photograph Dahlia had pulled out of the scrapbook. The writing on the back had said *L. Rogers*. But Brooke didn't think he could be the man in the photograph. He was *old*, but not *that* old, unless their dating was wrong.

She wondered though…was this a family affair? From

the Rogers in the picture, to Jen Rogers. With this man as a link in between? One Leon Rogers to another? The family business of murder and hiding out in caves?

"I don't suppose you have any relation to Jen Rogers?" she asked, trying to keep everything light and conversational. No doubt the deputies would be working to get her out of this cave. She only had to keep herself safe and sound until they did.

She hoped.

"Oh, Jen. My disappointment." Leon shook his head. "She never understood the history. Never respected our fate, or godliness." He put his palms together, pointed his finger up to the cave ceiling. "She only ever focused on her anger. Death isn't anger. It's freedom. You see, we're just freedom fighters down here. She never understood. She used it, tainted this, and she never understood."

"That's...too bad," Brooke said, trying to sound sympathetic even as fear slithered through her.

She had dealt with a lot of terrifying situations in her life, and perhaps this wasn't the most dangerous, but being trapped in a cave with a man who thought murder was freedom was certainly the most bizarre and left her feeling the most out of her element.

She *could* survive this, she knew, but she didn't have the first idea as to *how*. Yet.

"Have you...dealt with a cave-in like this before?" she asked, trying to sound bright and unaffected by the way he stared at her. The way all of this was so deeply and horribly unsettling.

She knew other entrances existed. The marked ones in the preserve, then other ones not usually big enough for people. Just wildlife.

Did he use any of those, or did he really just live in here?

With all these bones. In all this darkness? But he had fire. He'd survived. Surely he had some outside life. *Surely.*

He clucked his tongue. "The cave doesn't treat me that way. I am its god."

"Ah." What was there to say to that?

"*I* did that."

Brooke blinked. "You...caused the cave-in?"

"Of course. It's been so long since I've had a good one. I'm getting too old and feeble. But you're stuck now. I just needed you stuck. You don't carry a gun like they do."

Brooke swallowed and balled her hands into fists so her shakes weren't visible, she hoped. "A gun isn't the only weapon a person has."

There were her tools, for starters, if she could get to them. He hadn't gotten that far inside the room yet. She could get there and grab one before he could stop her, probably, considering how old he was.

But if she ran for one now, she'd be too close to him. She definitely didn't want to be too close to him. Maybe he was old, maybe she could overpower him, but he seemed so calm. Like he had some kind of secret.

"The cave brought you to me," he said, moving closer. "You are its offering. Why don't you sit and accept your fate?"

Okay, this was getting worse. But he *was* old and feeble. And she didn't see any weapon yet. So why would she accept *any* fate? She was young and strong and capable. She could fight her way out of this, no matter how ill-suited she was to fighting.

Or so she thought. He dropped his torch and the flame went out with a sizzle.

Then he pulled out a gun.

Chapter Eighteen

Zeke didn't like how long it was taking to walk to the back of the cave. The map had made it look like a short distance, but this was taking too long. Or maybe he was too impatient, thinking of Brooke sitting in that cave alone. Possibly trapped—on purpose.

His training told him to turn off all thoughts of Brooke. Bank those emotions and deal with reality. He didn't know if it was age, years out of North Star, or the depth of his feelings for Brooke, but he just couldn't manage it. His pace kept picking up.

Luckily, they hadn't encountered anyone yet. Not random hikers or campers and, more importantly, no law enforcement. That led Zeke to believe rescue efforts were focused on the front side of the cave.

So theirs would focus on the back.

"Do you think Chloe will let you know if they get her out of there?"

"Yeah, she'll probably send me a text, but I don't know if I'll get it with the patchy service," Carlyle replied.

Well, then he'd try to convince himself Brooke was fine and they just hadn't gotten the message. He'd slow his pace. Be careful and tactical.

"They ever teach you stealth in the Sons?" Zeke grumbled since Royal seemed bound and determined to rush ahead even worse than him, being loud enough that anyone might know they're coming.

"I wasn't *in* the Sons," Royal returned. "I was *infiltrating* the Sons and lived to tell the tale. I've got plenty of stealth."

"Maybe use it," Carlyle muttered, her eyes moving around the trees that surrounded them.

Zeke didn't mind their bickering. It kind of reminded him of being back in North Star. There was a certain level of…levity you had to maintain when dealing with such serious situations. It was like falling back into old familiar patterns. But not…going back in time. More a nostalgic feeling.

Something he was grateful to have in his past. Not necessarily something he wanted to go back to. And that was… new.

But he didn't have time to think about that, to consider what it really meant, because a little prickle started at the base of his neck and he heard something…off in the trees around them.

Zeke held up a hand. Something or someone was out there. Rescue personnel headed for the back cave entrance? Or a threat—to them or to Brooke? He had never heard of any cave-ins at this cave, and if Jen Rogers had lived there for years, undetected like they'd claimed, he doubted any cave-in was *natural.*

Both Royal and Carlyle stopped on a dime, everyone holding up their guns and surveying the area. Carlyle, knowing the drill, moved back-to-back with Zeke.

Royal caught on quick and moved so they stood in a defensive position, facing out, backs protected.

Zeke heard it again. The crack of a twig. Could be an animal but...

A man stepped out from behind a few trees. He wore jeans and a hoodie and hiking boots. He didn't appear to be carrying a weapon, but he grinned. Right at Royal.

"Long time no see."

He didn't carry a gun, and now had three trained on him, but was far too cheerful to not have a trick up his sleeve.

"Vince," Royal returned, acting as relaxed and belligerent as he had when Zeke had first met him, even with a gun pointed at the new arrival. "Fancy meeting you in Wyoming. Didn't think you ever climbed out of the sludge in South Dakota."

"You've recruited some friends, Royal." The man shook his head. "Too bad for them."

Another former member of the Sons. Clearly. No doubt part of the threat against Brooke, thanks to Royal. Had he caused the cave-in? Was this really *all* about Royal and the Sons? It didn't add up, but Zeke wouldn't put anything past a bunch of embittered criminals.

"You'd be surprised who it'll be too bad for," Carlyle returned, always running her mouth.

"So would you, babe." The man took his gaze from Carlyle to Royal. "You made a lot of enemies that day." As if that was the cue, three other men—all with guns—stepped out from around the cave entrance they'd been heading for. "Time to pay up."

"You guys don't have an independent thought of your own. Always have to be following some vindictive leader. What do you think my father is going to do for you while he's locked up?" Royal demanded.

"I don't think that's any of your business, traitor."

"There's nothing to betray," Royal responded with an impressive amount of calm Zeke had to give him credit for. "Y'all were held together by a psychopath, and he's dead. Everything else is blown to hell. Why don't you just go live your lives? Why concern yourself with old pointless business?"

For a moment, the ringleader simply blinked, like that had never occurred to him. Then he scoffed. "We're our own group now. Stronger than anything Wyatt ever did. Loyal to Jeremiah Campbell."

Zeke laughed. Couldn't help himself. Ace Wyatt had been a psychopath, albeit a brilliant one. He'd wielded his brand of sadism and cunning to form a powerful gang for *decades*. Whatever these four were involved in, it was nothing like the Sons.

"I've never even *heard* of Jeremiah Campbell," Zeke offered. "And I've personally taken down more Sons members than some low-level lackey like you have probably ever met."

This ticked off all four of the men, based on their expressions, but the three with guns didn't start shooting. So they stood in a ridiculous standoff here in the middle of a nature preserve.

"You'll see," the unarmed guy offered with a sneer.

"Yeah, I bet," Royal said. "So, what? You're just going to have a shootout here? And then what? Disappear?"

"Disappearing is our specialty."

"Imagine this guy thinking he has a specialty," Carlyle said, pretending she was making a throwaway comment to Zeke and Royal rather than addressing the guy specifically.

"You know cops are crawling all over this preserve,

right? One shot fired and you'll be done for in no time," Royal said.

"No Sons to wriggle you out of jail time now, is there?" Zeke added. "Your 'better' group got a passel of lawyers and paid-off cops lined up? Because that was Ace Wyatt's real specialty, as I recall."

"Don't you know about this cave?" Vince said, jerking a thumb behind him where the back entrance to the cave was not too far away. "People who disappear here don't come out, and hey, if you and your friends here were looking for your sister, why wouldn't you get turned around and just...*poof.*" He made a little hand gesture to go with the sound effect.

"Guess you better start shooting then," Carlyle said. "See who winds up on top." She dramatically flicked the safety off her gun.

Hell. She never did have any patience. So Zeke followed suit, wondering how he was going to keep all three of them from getting shot.

BROOKE STAYED FROZEN. Leon just stood there, gun pointed at her, though his arm was starting to shake. She didn't know how to get out of this. He blocked the only exit she knew of—with a gun.

She *could* knock him over, and he very well *could* miss shooting her since he was hardly holding the weapon steady. But was it worth the chance? Shot by accident was the same as on purpose when all was said and done.

But there was a slight discrepancy here. "You don't kill your victims with a gun." She hadn't gone through all the remains in this cave, but aside from the ones Jen had confessed to, no remains had showed any evidence of a gunshot wound.

He raised his eyebrows then gave a nod like she was quite right. "You've been studying my prizes. So, how do I do it then?"

Brooke pressed her palms to the cold, wet rock behind her. She used that as a kind of centering. She was still alive. There was still hope. Just keep him talking until she got out. People knew she was in here. They were working to get her out. Not just people. *Police officers*. With guns of their own.

"With the age of the remains I've dated and studied, my guess would be starvation or terminal dehydration is your preferred method."

Again he nodded, like a professor proud of a student for getting a difficult question *partially* right. "Sometimes we found them that way. An offering from the cave. And sometimes Father and I worked as a team." He smiled fondly. "My father was a good partner. He understood the god. The offering. My daughter…" He shook his head and the smile died. "I went through a dark period when she was my partner. It's better alone again."

"That section over there." Brooke pointed to the second quadrant. The one she'd just begun to study. "I haven't gotten very far, but I've found more broken bones than this quadrant."

"Mmm." Leon studied her but didn't offer anything else.

"So, you were more violent with those victims?" Brooke prompted.

"Stop calling them that." His mouth turned into a scowl, his nostrils flared. Anger seeped into his expression. "Not victims. Offerings. Prizes. For me. God of the cave." The scowl curved back up into a psychotic grin that turned her blood to ice. "Violent, maybe. But broken bones don't kill, do they?"

"They can."

"But did they? That's the question."

"I haven't studied that portion enough to know," she hedged. "It takes time. To study. To excavate. To discern." She glanced at the wall behind her. She didn't hear anything coming from the other side. Had more deputies been trapped? Hurt? Was it worse on the other side?

Brooke looked back at Leon. He pointed to her bag that still sat next to the quadrant she'd been working on. "Take your tools. Tell me."

She didn't want to do anything that he told her, but if she got her tools, she had a weapon. Maybe it wasn't a *gun*, but it was something. She moved forward, keeping a careful eye on him so she knew she was always out of reach. She did her best to keep that gun from pointing directly at her as she gathered her bag of tools. She moved over to the quadrant she'd only just begun.

There could have been a lot of reasons the bones in this sector were more broken over here. It could have meant a violent means of death or something more environmental. She wasn't far enough in her excavation and research to know for sure.

If she dragged this out, took her time, surely someone would be able to get to her by then. No matter what things looked like on the other side of that pile of rocks, too many people knew where she was. People who would save her. The police. Zeke. Her brother. She wasn't going to wither away here.

As long as she survived whatever Leon was up to. So she turned her attention back to the ground beneath her. She had to excavate. Slowly. Much more slowly than even she usually went. Time was her best weapon. She'd have to use it.

Brooke got to work, trying to block out Leon's existence, or why she was doing this. Just fooling herself into thinking it was any other workday. Uncover a bone here, another bone. Carefully. She didn't take pictures like she usually did, but Laurel had been the one with the camera and, well, anyone could forgive her for not attempting that in her current circumstances.

After a while, she became aware of his hot breath on her neck. She tried to breathe through the wave of nausea that swamped her. Tried not to let her hands shake. She didn't remove any of the bones, just uncovered them as they were laid out. Legs to hips to rib cage to…

"What do you think?" he asked just as she uncovered the neck.

Brooke swallowed so her voice would sound calm and clear. So she didn't shudder at the nearness of him.

"I'd need to run tests. I'd need my lab. I can't tell just by looking." Of course she had enough experience to make an educated guess. Broken neck.

Was that what he wanted her to say? But she forgot everything when something wet and sticky touched *her* neck, like a tongue, and on a shriek, she jumped up. Halfway through the knee-jerk reaction, she chose to use it to her advantage. She flung her head back as she came up, the top of her skull crashing into his chin, his frail body stumbling backward. The gun he'd been holding landed on the ground with a dull thud.

Brooke made a dive for the gun, not allowing herself to think about anything else, but she crashed into him trying to do the same. Something he did caused one of the lights to topple over, making a popping sound as it went dark.

He cackled with delight as they both got a grip on the gun at the same time. She ripped it out of his weak grasp, but he must have known she would. Or maybe everything was just against her—because the last light toppled over.

And they were plunged into utter darkness.

Brooke didn't panic...at first. She got to her feet, curled her hand around the weapon and adjusted it until she had it in a shooting position. She tried to feel around for the safety, but she didn't know what kind of gun it was and couldn't find it.

Maybe he didn't have it on. She curled her finger around the trigger, and then tried to decide what to do.

From far too close, a gurgling cackle echoed around her.

And she couldn't see where to go. Or where to shoot.

Chapter Nineteen

Brooke forced herself to breathe. Terror and panic clawed through her. She was frozen in place—which wasn't so bad when surrounded by nothing but a deep, black nothingness.

But she had a weapon. She had a gun. She didn't know if it was loaded or even capable of shooting, but it was something to hold on to.

Once she'd calmed herself enough that she could hear over the roaring beat of panic inside her body, she heard the sound of shuffling. Of rattling breathing. She was still, but Leon was moving around.

Was he trying to find her? Did he have some sort of ability to see in all this black? Wouldn't he stumble and fall in the dips and holes and cave growth? Or was he just so used to it, none of that mattered?

She took in her surroundings again. Surely it wasn't *totally* dark. There'd been an opening not too far away, right? The cave-in couldn't have completely covered the entrance. If she could find that, she could orient herself.

She squinted. Was that a tiny pinpoint of light? Or was she hallucinating? Could that possibly be the caved-in entrance? If it was, then directly behind her would take her deeper into the cave and potentially to another entrance.

Did she dare risk it? Without a light?

Well, standing still and waiting to be saved hadn't gotten her anywhere. She didn't even *hear* people trying to save her. Why not *do* something for once?

Carefully, she turned, making sure she did a complete one-eighty from the pinpoint of light. She paused, listening for Leon. He sounded…far away? Maybe? Or was that just wishful thinking?

You have a gun. You're stronger. No matter what, you can survive this. You are a survivor. Maybe she'd endured more than survived, but she wasn't about to *endure* her death. No way.

She used that as a mantra to keep her thoughts from spiraling to worst-case scenarios. She moved forward one step, carefully feeling the ground with her toe before putting any weight on her foot. It would be a meticulous, long process, but she was used to that kind of thing, wasn't she?

After each step, she paused, listened, tried to ensure Leon wasn't too close. After a while, on one of her pauses, she heard a scratch of something like…the flare of a match being lit. She whirled around, trying to find the light it should make.

She saw just the wink of flame and then it was gone. It had outlined something shadowy, but large. Taller than Leon. Was someone else in this cave with them, or was she losing her mind?

Brooke stopped moving. Held her breath, waiting for something else to happen as her heart pounded.

This time when a light flashed on, it wasn't a match or a torch. It was the beam of a flashlight.

It illuminated the man in front of her—closer than she would have guessed. Bloody and wild-eyed. But Leon didn't have a weapon, even as he smirked his horrible rotted-teeth grin at her.

"I am the god of the cave!" he shouted, raising his hands above his head. Then he sank to his knees. And someone was behind him, jerking his hands back.

A someone she recognized, even if it took a minute to understand what was happening in front of her.

"Granger."

She couldn't believe her eyes. The only man who'd ever been a father figure in her life was tying Leon's hands and then ankles together.

He left him there and walked over to Brooke.

"Are you okay?" he asked, reaching out to take her arm.

She nearly collapsed into him. She didn't even ask how he'd found her. How he'd gotten here. But she knew she was safe now. He'd saved her, and not for the first time.

"Come on, Brooke," he said, pulling her around Leon's laughing body. "Let's get you out of here."

THE GUNSHOT CAME out of nowhere.

Zeke hadn't fired, and the noise wasn't close enough to be Royal or Carlyle's shooting.

Then Royal went down with a jerk and a stumble. Zeke whirled in time with Carlyle, but the shooter didn't even try to hide. He walked through the trees with confident strides, gun held loosely. Zeke could have taken him out, but he had no doubt he'd earn three bullets from behind if he did.

"Hold," Zeke muttered to Carlyle, afraid she'd start shooting and get them both killed. Right now, they were outnumbered and they had to be careful if they were going to get out of this. He edged toward Royal, who was at least moving around. Wherever he'd been hit wasn't a fatal wound. Not yet.

"Never met me, huh?" the gunman said to Zeke. "Maybe North Star hotshots weren't as tough as they thought."

So this was Brooke and Royal's father. Not in jail. If Zeke had to guess, based on the four men surrounding them, Jeremiah Campbell was trying his hand at cobbling together some new offshoot of the Sons. He was hardly the first. In his time with North Star, Zeke had helped take down at least two attempts and had known of at least three other cases.

But what these men had never understood was that any association with the Sons put a mark on their backs. Connection to the Sons no longer meant the power they thought it did. And thanks to Granger, and everyone who'd ever worked at North Star, they never would again.

Zeke had always been proud of his work at North Star, but he hadn't been too thrilled when the group had disbanded. For selfish reasons, he realized now. Because it took this moment to understand all they had done by stopping a powerful group of men who'd hurt untold numbers of people.

Brooke and Royal included.

"Thought you were in jail," Royal said from between clenched teeth, echoing Zeke's thoughts. Blood seeped from Royal's arm, but he was conscious. That was something. And *someone* looking for Brooke had to have heard the gunshot. They'd come searching.

Had to.

"The idea that anyone working those jails knows anything that's going on." Jeremiah laughed. "I'm sure everyone thinks that's exactly where I am, but I've always been smarter than the system."

Zeke laughed. "Ah, yes. That's why you landed in jail in the first place. *Smarts*."

"I have missed going toe to toe with North Star's brain-less soldiers."

"And losing? Because we literally had to disband. We'd eradicated the whole Sons network and there was nothing left to do. Because without your psychopath leader, you are literally *nothing*."

"And yet here I am. Outnumbering *you*."

He wasn't wrong about that, but Zeke didn't concern himself with being outnumbered. He'd been there done that a hundred times. His biggest concern right now was that he couldn't take the time he'd like to draw this out. Royal needed medical attention.

So, they had to get this show on the road. He wasn't about to let Brooke's brother bleed out on his watch.

Zeke raised his gun, pointing it directly at Jeremiah. "Guess we're at a crossroads then."

Chapter Twenty

Granger held on to her and led her deeper into the cave. His flashlight helped them not trip over anything, but the dark around the beam of light somehow felt more oppressive as they moved along a cold, wet cave wall.

But he was here, and Brooke had help. She still couldn't get over it. "Why did you come?"

"I was in the area."

She scowled at his back. "Granger."

"It's a long story. We'll get it sorted soon enough. Look, right ahead." He pointed and she saw the little sliver of natural light.

Almost there. She could *cry*. Or just collapse. But she didn't let herself do either. Getting out was only one step. Then they had to deal with the aftermath. Find the police and tell them about Leon, get back into that cave and collect the necessary evidence and so forth.

But, man, all she really wanted was to go home.

And she didn't let herself think too deeply about the fact she didn't *have* a home, but when she thought about one, she pictured Zeke's half-renovated house. Viola. *Him*.

It took longer than she'd expected to get to the entrance, but they finally did. It felt blinding to step out into the sunlight, and she had to squeeze her eyes shut. Granger held tight to her, and she still didn't know how this was possible. This whole weird day.

"You didn't have to come."

He laughed. "Only you would say that to me after I saved your butt, Brooke."

She managed to blink her eyes open and not immediately shut them against the brightness. "It's not that I'm ungrateful."

"You don't want to put me out. I know. I wish you'd get it through your head you're not a burden to us. Any of us." That was not the first time he'd said that to her, but maybe it was the first time she was really taking it on board.

She didn't know what had changed. No, that was a lie. She knew it was Zeke calling her out on not wanting to be a burden. It was Zeke, period. It shouldn't be about him. No matter what he'd done or said, he didn't love her. Not really.

But he'd jumped in to help after all this time. He'd claimed he'd changed, that his roots could be hers, and she didn't feel so afraid with him that she was...well, what Granger had said. Some kind of *burden*.

Something on Granger's phone beeped and he frowned at it. But he smoothed out that frown quickly. He pointed to a trail outside the cave.

"Follow that path and you'll find the rescue team. They've been focused on the west entrance. You can tell them I helped, or say you handled it yourself. I'll back up the story either way."

He even gave her a little nudge in that direction while he moved in the other.

Brooke stared at him in confusion. "Where are you going?"

He paused a second, looked in the opposite direction

of the trail then at his watch. Gauging something, though she couldn't tell what. When he looked at her, his expression was the stern kind of North Star taskmaster she hadn't seen in a while. Because they weren't North Star anymore. "I started looking into Royal, your father, the lawyer, after your and Zeke's call. I don't like what I've found out about your father, Brooke. The ties he might have, and what he might have people doing for him. I'm just going to go make sure everything is good on some of those loose ends."

"That doesn't explain *where* you're going."

"I think I've got a lead on who put that explosive in your car, the tracker in Royal's. I was working on that when we got word of the cave-in. Go find the rescue team, Brooke. Your head's bleeding. I'll handle this."

"Handle *what*?"

He sighed. "Look. There's a little group of guys that have a prison connection to your father. I think they were after you but got…sidetracked when the cave-in happened and they couldn't easily get to you."

"Sidetracked by *what*?"

He looked up at the sky and shook his head. "Fine. Sidetracked by Royal himself. And Zeke. And a woman, I'm assuming that's Zeke's sister."

Brooke immediately turned away from the trail. "I'm going with you."

"Brooke. You've got a rescue squad looking for you, and this is dangerous. You've got a gash on your head. Go get checked out and—"

"You trained me yourself, Granger. Self-defense. How to shoot. If I can help, I should."

"When was the last time you practiced any kind of

shooting? I've got a few people coming. No worries, Brooke. I can handle it."

He could. Probably. But she was always letting someone else *handle it*. Hiding in caves with remains that couldn't do anything to her. "I'm not going to leave Royal on his own again. I can't abandon him."

"You never did, Brooke. You were a kid."

She hated that he knew her this well. That, aside from Zeke, Granger and his wife and a few other North Star people were the only ones who did. Because she could fool anyone else.

But not family.

"Maybe you're right, but I'm not doing it now. I can't... always be saved. At some point, I have to be part of the saving."

"He's not alone. We've got this handled."

"He's my brother, Granger."

He sighed heavily. "Why'd I recruit all these stubborn mules?" he muttered. He glanced at his watch. "Gabriel should be here any minute. Reece not far behind. Shay had to stay with the kids, and that was a fight and a half. But I've got Betty on standby at her insistence just in case anything gets hairy. She can patch you up. Come on."

Brooke followed him carefully through the trees, the gun from Leon still in her hand. Gabriel and Reece were former North Star operatives like Zeke. Reece had gotten out himself almost before she'd joined up, so she didn't know him that well. Gabriel had been around a lot during her time and had been there at the end. He'd even married Zeke's cousin, Mallory, who'd gotten Zeke into North Star. Brooke *had* been close to Betty, who was North Star's resident doctor. Since the support staff people had spent a lot of time together, and as Betty and Brooke had both been interested in medical science, it had been a quick and easy friendship.

Though, like with most North Star people, Brooke hadn't kept in good touch, not wanting to bother anyone. Always feeling a little "other" once North Star had disbanded and so many had gone on to start lives and families.

But that was the thing. All these people were married, many with kids. Granger had a wife and a ton of foster kids at home. Reece had a wife and a stepson and, if Brooke recalled correctly, a few more kids since. She didn't know if Gabriel and Mallory had a family, but *still*. Betty had married a sheriff and moved to Montana to help raise his twins, last Brooke knew.

They'd all gotten away from the danger of North Star because of those families, those choices.

"Granger. You don't have to be doing this. I can… I'll handle the stuff with Royal. You all should go home."

"Home," he said, shaking his head. "Home is family, Brooke. And that's what we are. With or without North Star, we're all family. No matter how anybody feels about it. Forever." He gave a glance over her shoulder then pointed through the trees. "Reece is over there. He's watching something. We're going to approach silently, okay? Don't make a sound."

She nodded. She could do that. She might not be good at the whole operative-and-handling-danger thing, but she knew how to follow orders. And she *did* know how to shoot the gun she carried now that she could see it.

She would help. Whatever this was, she was finally going to help Royal. No matter what he'd gotten himself into.

She followed Granger cautiously until Reece's careful

hiding spot came into view. He'd created a natural kind of trench with some fallen logs and a rock outcropping. Brooke and Granger joined him behind the barrier.

They all crouched low and spoke in barely-there whispers.

"Five men, four armed. Surrounding Royal, Zeke and an unknown woman." Reece flicked Brooke a look and then one at Granger, who gave a little go-ahead nod.

"Royal's been shot, but he's awake," Reece continued, handing Granger a pair of binoculars. "He's alert. Betty's on standby, not far off. Minute we can, we'll get him to her."

All that fear Brooke had let go once Granger had appeared crept back in. Her brother had been *shot*. He and Zeke and Carlyle were surrounded by *five* people. She didn't dare peek over the barrier. She just had to…deal.

But not alone. Not hiding. Together.

Family.

ZEKE WAS PREPARED to get shot. Hell, he'd survived it a few times, he could do it again. He didn't let himself dwell on the errant thought that here he was in a standoff, finally *not* having a death wish, and he just might get himself killed.

Nah. Not today. He had to make Brooke believe they could make this work. Couldn't check out now. He wasn't going to let this end in any way she might blame herself.

Just then, as if on some cosmic cue, far off but distinct, Zeke heard a whistle. A North Star whistle. Then he saw the glint of something—a gun. And he recognized the hand making a gesture from behind a tree. Walker.

"Cops," Carlyle whispered. "Behind us."

Backup. All different kinds. Zeke grinned.

He aimed his weapon right at Jeremiah Campbell. "Took down too many men like you in my life. Won't faze me to do it again."

Jeremiah must have sensed something because he looked behind him. Walker and Cash stepped out from their hiding places. Both held guns. But before Jeremiah could even react to that, the sounds of heavy footfalls reached them.

"Drop your weapons," Hart shouted, cresting a hill. Gun drawn, with Chloe Brink not far behind. Both in their Bent County uniforms.

"Now," she added.

The man who hadn't had a gun took off running, while two of the gunmen dropped their weapons. Another held on to his and ran. Jeremiah just stood there. Fuming while the North Star contingent quickly stopped the attempted runners.

Reece Montgomery and Gabriel Saunders each took out a gunman, while Cash's brother, Palmer, took out the other.

A convergence of the different facets of his life. All coming together to help. Protect. Save.

Then there was Brooke. She had some crusted blood on her temple but didn't look to be actively bleeding. And she rushed to Royal's side. He wanted to run to her too, but he let her have the moment with her brother while Granger texted Betty to come on down and Hart radioed for an ambulance.

Zeke gave one more glance at Jeremiah. Walker and Cash had guns trained on him while Chloe moved over with a pair of handcuffs. She kept telling him to drop his weapon, but he hadn't yet.

So Zeke walked over.

Jeremiah didn't lift his gun, but he lifted his chin. "You're on my list."

Zeke reached forward and grabbed the gun out of Jeremiah's hand before the man even had a chance to react. North Star training at its finest. He handed it to Chloe. "I'm on everyone you know's list," Zeke returned. "And I still sleep soundly at night because you all are nothing. Always have been."

Chloe cuffed the man and then jerked him away. More cops were appearing, dragging the now-handcuffed perpetrators back toward the road where, hopefully, cruisers were waiting to take them to the sheriff's office.

Because all of these people had come together to help, to do the right thing, to protect each other. Against a small contingent of people who'd worked together to hurt and harm.

Zeke's childhood had been marked by the inability to save his mother against men like that and, like so many realizations lately, this one hit him out of the blue.

He'd spent most of his adult life trying to make that all right. Solve it, like it was a problem. When all it had ever been was a tragedy. One that he'd had no control over.

Not his fault.

Walker pounded him on the shoulder. "What the hell?"

Zeke shook his head. "Didn't know what we were getting ourselves into. How'd you find us?"

Walker jerked a thumb at Cash.

Carlyle's fiancé shrugged. "Carlyle and I track each other's locations. When she disappeared, I figured she'd gone to see you, but after a while I realized she wouldn't let you hit the cave alone. But when the cops hadn't seen you guys, we checked it to see where she was. Lost service here and there, so couldn't pinpoint an exact location at first, but we got close, then your friend found us."

Zeke scoured the scene. Granger and Gabriel stood just a ways back from where Brooke knelt next to Royal. Betty was with her, clearly working on Royal.

She was okay. *Okay.*

Carlyle sauntered over, wrapped an arm around Cash's waist but looked up at Zeke. "Just going to stand there staring at her?"

Zeke scowled at his sister. "Giving her a minute with her *injured* brother."

"Give her a *shoulder*, dipshit. They're going to cart him out of here the minute they get a stretcher in. She's going to need support."

When Zeke didn't immediately jump to action, Carlyle made a disgusted sound. "If she walks out on you, you damn well deserve it." Then she gave him a physical push with her free hand.

Zeke grumbled, but he moved over to the scene around Royal. They had him up in a sitting position and Betty had already wrapped a bandage around his arm.

"Nice save," Zeke offered to his old boss.

Granger shrugged. "Only because you two got me started on looking into that lawyer Brooke paid. Led me to Jeremiah, which didn't sit right. Started keeping tabs on a guy who visited the alleged Jeremiah in jail weekly without fail and that led me here."

Two EMTs with a stretcher appeared and gently but firmly moved Brooke out of the way. Zeke reached out and helped her to her feet. Once she looked up at him, she simply fell into him.

He wrapped his arms around her, held her. Up to this point, he'd kept every feeling as much on lockdown as he could, but too many rushed through him now with her in his arms. The kind of relief that threatened to buckle his knees.

"Everything's okay," he told her, holding her close. "Everyone's going to be just fine."

She nodded into his chest. "He'll be okay," she said, and he knew she was saying it to reassure herself, not because she knew it was true. But it would be true.

They were all going to be okay. He rubbed a hand down her back and promised himself he'd make sure of it.

Chapter Twenty-One

The detectives let Zeke give her a ride to the hospital, but Brooke wasn't allowed to see Royal right away. Instead, she had to let a nurse poke and prod at her head, then bandage her up. Once she was done with that, she had to answer what felt like a zillion questions from Laurel in a meeting room at the hospital. About what happened in the cave.

Brooke really hated recounting it. She would no doubt have nightmares about Leon Rogers for some time. And she still had work to do down there. With three murderers spanning three generations…no telling what unsolved disappearances she might be able to help solve.

"So how does all of that connect to what happened on the outside?" Laurel said, turning her attention to Zeke, who held Brooke's hand under the table they were sitting at.

He hadn't left her side. Hadn't gone more than a few seconds without having one of his hands touching her in some way. It gave her the strength to go on when what she really wanted was to curl up somewhere and sleep forever.

Except when she closed her eyes, she still pictured Leon and shivered.

"I don't actually think there's a connection," Brooke said before Zeke could. "Two separate issues just happened to merge."

"I agree with that assessment," Zeke said. "The problem people I ran into were connected to her brother, his old life. They wanted to use Brooke as a kind of revenge. I think they were following her, waiting for a chance to get to her. When the cave-in happened and we came to try and help, we just happened to run into them trying to get to her."

Laurel rubbed a hand to her temple. "This is a hell of a case, you guys. That should hold us over for now. I'm sure we'll have more questions as the case—cases—continue, but if you want to go check on your brother, Brooke, we're done here."

They all stood, and Laurel gave her a friendly pat on the back. "Get some rest, Brooke. You did good today."

Brooke managed a smile. "You too, Detective."

They all left the meeting room and Brooke couldn't stop herself from leaning on Zeke. He seemed to be the only thing holding her up. She wanted to be stronger than that, but...

Well, for once, it was nice to be so tired she didn't worry about leaning on someone, didn't worry about being a burden. Because Zeke was here of his own volition, just like everyone else today, helping because they *wanted* to. Because they cared.

"Granger texted me where to go," Zeke said, leading her down one hallway and then into the next. They finally reached one where Brooke saw a familiar face.

Betty moved forward and enveloped her in a hug. "He's just fine," she reassured. "The doctor will run you through all the aftercare you'll have to do, but he's lucky it wasn't more serious."

"Thank you for being there."

Betty pulled back. "Anytime. It's good to see you, Brooke."

"You too." And Brooke meant that, even if she didn't know how to convey it. Not when she was so tired. Achy. Hungry. Someone had tried to get her to eat, but she couldn't stomach the thought.

"You should be able to talk to him now." Betty opened the door to Royal's room. "We'll catch up more when you're done."

Brooke nodded and stepped into Royal's hospital room. He watched her get close, smiled wryly. "Hey, Chick."

"Hey yourself." She crossed to his bed.

"I'm fine. Really." He pointed to her head with his good arm. "What about that?"

"Just a scratch," she said, touching the bandage. "No concussion. I'm good."

"Best-case scenario all in all, then, huh?"

She couldn't agree with that because she didn't like him hurt, but he was okay. He was alive. This was all... sorted. No more danger. No more... Sons or their father.

But where did that leave them? Her baby brother she didn't know. She wanted to protect him now, but if he was safe, and an adult...

So she just...let herself be a burden to him. Because she loved him, he was her brother, her family. Maybe it wasn't a burden to ask for something. Maybe it was just love.

"I hope you won't disappear on me, Royal. I hope that we can...be each other's family again." She blinked back tears and tried to ignore how horrible it felt to be so... vulnerable. To admit she wanted him around. "You don't have to—"

"Chick."

A tear escaped, but she blinked back the rest. Royal

reached out and took her hand in his. "You're the only family I got. And it's not your fault I messed that up. I blamed you all those years because… Well, maybe there's no real reason. I was a dumb kid and it felt like everyone else had it better. Even you. Maybe especially you, because I know you deserved it. And I didn't."

"We didn't deserve any of it, Royal."

"Maybe not all. But I made… I'm not like you, Brooke. I've made some real mistakes. Maybe I didn't deserve all that jail time, but I'm no saint."

"You could reform."

He grimaced then gave a little snort of a laugh. "Reform might be a stretch, but I could probably try out not breaking any laws. And to keep in touch, no matter where we end up."

"It'd be a start."

"It's a promise."

Another tear escaped and she wiped it away. She leaned over. Brushed a kiss across his forehead like she used to do when she was comforting him in the midst of something terrible when they'd been kids lost in a really awful world.

But this wasn't terrible anymore. This was the start of something good. She was determined.

A nurse came in with a kind smile. "We need some privacy to run some tests. Visiting hours are coming to an end tonight anyway. But you can come back tomorrow, of course."

Brooke nodded.

"Go on back to Zeke's, Chick. I'll call you in the morning when they let me out. Promise."

Brooke let out a long, slow breath. She was going to choose to believe that promise. That one, and one for the future. Of her brother back in her life. *Family*. The blood kind.

And all the ones she'd built out there.

She exited Royal's room and Betty was still standing there.

Brooke just wanted to go *home*. But so many people had come to help her. She felt like she had to reach out across that effort, because she'd cut it off.

"Thanks for patching him up, Betty."

"Anytime."

"So, do I get to see pictures of your little ones or do I have to beg?"

Betty didn't hesitate. She pulled out her phone. Scrolled through picture after picture of two adorable toddlers and their handsome father doing all sorts of things—playing in the snow, messily eating spaghetti, just lying on the couch.

An odd ache settled in Brooke's chest. It was lovely and she was so happy for Betty, who was no doubt an exceptional mother.

Every picture was just so homey. All things…well, things Brooke had never had. And now she wanted. She glanced at Zeke, who stood down the hall talking to Granger. They were both serious, but not worried. Not heavy with concern. Likely just going over any last details.

As if Betty could read her thoughts, she nodded toward the two. "You and Zeke again, huh?"

Brooke shouldn't be making any decisions after such a day. She should get some sleep and just…get her head on straight before she dealt with *her and Zeke*. "I… I don't know."

"Yes, you do." Betty patted her on the shoulder.

Zeke happened to look over, offered her a smile.

Well, she supposed she did.

ZEKE'S HOUSE WAS full of North Star people. It had been late by the time they'd gotten done with questioning, and while it wasn't five-star accommodations, it was better than some of their old missions. Besides, it was one night. Everyone would be off again in the morning, back to the lives they'd built.

When Zeke finally got bed assignments sorted, he returned to the kitchen to find Brooke doing dishes of all things. With that bandage on her face and dark circles under her eyes. Because it was late, and she'd been through hell.

"Well, I ran out of beds. You go on and take mine. I'll finish here."

She set the glass she'd been washing aside then looked at him with an expression he couldn't quite read. "That's a terrible pickup line."

He laughed in spite of himself. "I'm going to sleep on the *couch*, Brooke."

She shook her head, walked over to him and wrapped her arms around him, resting her head on his chest. "No, you're not."

He ran a hand over her hair, gave himself a moment to revel in the fact that she was in his arms. "Sweetheart, you need to rest."

"So do you."

He let out a long breath. Yeah, it had been a *day*. He moved his arm around her waist, started leading her toward his bedroom. Everything they had to talk about could wait. There was no rush. Not really. They could sleep in his bed, keep their hands to themselves, and deal with everything tomorrow.

Except so much could have happened today. So much *bad*, so much loss. If they hadn't had help. If they hadn't had each other.

So maybe wasting another second didn't make any sense.

He stopped, turned her to face him in the dim light of his living room. In a house he'd started renovating, convincing himself it was a just-for-the-hell-of-it project.

But surely it had always been for her.

"I love you, Brooke. I don't want you to go anywhere."

She studied him for the longest time. Long enough to start to make him feel...nervous. Long enough that he wanted to *fidget*.

"You really mean that, don't you?" she finally said.

He tucked a strand of hair behind her ear. "I'd never say it if I didn't. I never will."

Her smile eased every last worry inside him. "I love you too, Zeke."

"So you'll stay?"

She moved to her toes, pressed her mouth to his. "I'll stay," she murmured against his mouth.

And she did.

Forever.

Epilogue

A year later, when they got married in their fully renovated house on their *nearly* working ranch in Sunrise, Wyoming, all their different worlds came together for one perfect night.

Walkers. Hudsons. Daniels. Bent County detectives and North Star operatives. Kids all over the place.

Royal walked Brooke down the aisle, which made her cry. Granger stood up with Zeke, along with his brother, which made her cry harder.

She'd gone from being a lonely teen, desperate not to draw any attention to herself so she didn't get sent away, to a woman who had…so many different places to go, people to lean on. So much *love*.

And as she promised to love Zeke for the rest of her days, and he returned those same vows, she knew that no matter what threatened, they'd always fight it together.

Their whole, huge, cobbled-together family.

* * * * *